MOTHER, MAY I?

DIS

Look for other REMNANTS™
titles by K.A. Applegate:

#1 The Mayflower Project

#2 Destination Unknown

#3 Them

#4 Nowhere Land

#5 Mutation

#6 Breakdown

#7 Isolation

Also by K.A. Applegate:

 ®

REMNANTS™

MOTHER, MAY I?

K.A. APPLEGATE

AN
APPLE
PAPERBACK

SCHOLASTIC INC.
New York Toronto London Auckland Sydney
Mexico City New Delhi Hong Kong Buenos Aires

No part of this publication may be reproduced in whole or in part, or stored in a retrieval system, or transmitted in any form or by any means, electronic, mechanical, photocopying, recording, or otherwise, without written permission of the publisher. For information regarding permission, write to Scholastic Inc., Attention: Permissions Department, 557 Broadway, New York, NY 10012.

ISBN 0-590-88273-2

12 11 10 9 8 7 6 5 4 3 2 1   2 3 4 5 6 7/0

Printed in the U.S.A.   40
First Scholastic printing, September 2002

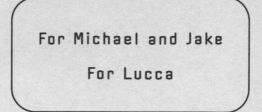

For Michael and Jake

For Lucca

MOTHER, MAY I?

2Face felt numb. Almost.

Tate and Tamara hadn't come down from the bridge. She'd heard Jobs say that they were alive, injured, just resting before joining the others.

Whatever.

Everyone else was gathered. Olga Gonzalez and Mo'Steel, her son. Jobs and his little brother, Edward. Violet. Dr. Cohen and Noyze. A phony, spaced-out Yago. D-Caf. A wounded Anamull. Roger Dodger. Kubrick. Burroway and T.R.

And Billy.

Something unbelievable had happened up on the bridge. Billy had defeated the psycho Baby/Shipwright/Maker.

Billy was the man of the moment. Their hero.

2Face felt the blood rise to her cheeks. Not numb anymore.

Spreading out from the base of the pyramidlike elevator, the fierce battle between the Riders and the Blue Meanies still raged. The Squids, Mother's backup defense team, had been pretty much decimated by the Meanies.

2Face watched the fighting. Billy might have destroyed the Baby/Shipwright/Maker, but was he powerful enough to stop the war?

"What's he doing?" Violet, from behind her.

2Face whirled. Billy was climbing the steps of the pyramid. 2Face watched in disbelief.

When he got to the top, he raised his arms and shouted: "Enough fighting!"

"We have to stop him!" Olga cried. "They'll kill him. Billy, get down!"

"Leave him alone," 2Face muttered.

Olga started to go after Billy. Mo'Steel stopped her. "Wait," he said quietly. "I think it's okay."

Billy drew his arms to his chest and closed his eyes. Just like that the Rider environment vanished.

2Face blinked. The hills, the copper-colored water, the weird trembling trees, the pink sky. It all just — gone.

In its place were two towering walls. Impossible. But, 2Face knew, all too real.

Everything and everyone, from humans to Riders to Meanies, were contained within the space defined by the massive walls.

The fighting stopped, just came to a dead halt.

"We're all going to have to figure this out!" Billy shouted.

Riders, Meanies, and humans drew closer to the base of the pyramid.

2Face felt someone's eyes on her. She turned. Mo'Steel. She stared at him, aware of the coldness in her own eyes.

Mo'Steel slowly averted his eyes.

2Face stayed where she was and let the others move in closer to Billy. Billy, who'd usurped all power. Billy, who'd staged a coup.

Only Yago stayed behind the crowd. He seemed oblivious to 2Face, to everyone. He stared up at Billy but 2Face saw that his eyes were unfocused. Yago and Billy, self-proclaimed rulers. If 2Face knew anything, she knew they hadn't heard the last of Yago's ambition to preside over Earth's few survivors.

Okay. Fine. So she'd find a way to deal with both of them. Strategically.

2Face was a self-preservationist of the highest order. She wasn't ashamed to admit that. And the best way to survive was to be the one who set down the guidelines for survival.

The real battle had just begun.

(CHAPTER ONE)

"YOU KNOW IT'S GOING TO
CAUSE TROUBLE, RIGHT?"

Three Months Later

Jobs was big.

This was helpful when you were on a quest through the immensity of space. It was also helpful to be able to travel at exhilarating speeds and unimagined velocities.

He was larger than the vast and various planets he passed. He could put his hand on a star, then right through it. He could peer closely at canyonlike craters and mile-high mountains and ten-mile-deep fissures as if he were the lens of a microscope and they were no larger than samples on a slide.

Worlds were his to examine, to evaluate, to own. Jobs collected solar systems like some people collected seashells. He noted one system's double sun, another system's huge gas-giant planets. He smiled at another's tiny moon.

Up here, out here with the stars and planets and

asteroids, Jobs sometimes felt like Gulliver from that old book written by a guy named Swift. *Gulliver's Travels*. In one place he'd gone, Gulliver found himself considered a giant in comparison to the local population who were about the size of his finger.

It was all about perspective in the end. Jobs knew he wasn't really as vast as a galaxy or as large as a solar system. But for the moment it seemed that he was. And that was all that mattered.

It was disturbing and it was wonderful.

Most of all, it was necessary. Because Jobs was determined to find a planet on which he and the other Remnants could settle. Life aboard Mother, though better since Billy had taken control, was not a long-term solution as far as Jobs was concerned.

And now he thought he might have found that habitable planet — and it seemed to be something he'd never dreamed he would find. He could go back there now, check it out. And part of him was relieved that Mo'Steel had come along this time for the ride.

"This is some kind of cool." Mo'Steel laughed as he jumped over a reddish medium-sized planet. "I am the monster-giant ruler of the universe! But virtual thrills are still just virtual, you know? Almost, but not quite. Can't feel it in my skin."

"Come on, man," Jobs said. He knew he sounded testy. "This is serious."

"Duck, you know you've been, uh, working, non-stop for, like, weeks. Maybe it's time for a little R and R. Lay back, relax, recharge the batteries."

"Can't."

"You know how many systems there are out here? A lot."

"A lot? Very precise, Mo."

"Ha-ha, 'migo. You know how long it takes you to decide if there's a livable planet in a given system? You want me to do the math for you?"

"I'm learning as I go," Jobs said. "I'm learning about what to look for."

And I think I've found it, Jobs said to himself. The question now: Was he ready to tell anyone what he'd seen?

The answer: Yes.

"Mo, you want to see something?"

"Sure. Is it awesomely amazing?"

"You tell me."

Jobs led Mo'Steel to another solar system. The journey took all of a second.

There was a big yellow star. There were eight planets. There was a spread of gas-giant planets, with the solid planets closer in.

This was the place.

"Why is everything so ... I don't know ... fuzzy?" Mo'Steel asked.

"I know. Poor visual resolution. This is the extreme limit of Mother's sensors," Jobs said. "It's the best picture she can get, basically. You have to see this. Look."

Jobs moved them closer to one of the planets.

It was a lumpish mess. It looked as if a larger planet had smashed into a smaller planet and both had been welded together in such a way as to preserve something of the two identities.

Small bodies of water were visible on the larger chunk, as well as a thin atmosphere and what looked to Jobs like some small, green areas.

The smaller chunk also had a thin atmosphere but no water or possible growth that Jobs could detect. Overall it was gray and pink and pockmarked with innumerable craters.

Jobs didn't say anything else. He waited for Mo'Steel to see it.

"Uh. Okay. Right. When did you find this?" Mo'Steel's voice was hushed.

"Last week. I didn't know what to do about it. Still don't." Jobs looked at his friend. "You know what this looks like, right?"

"Oh, yeah. Like a beat-up Earth with a broken-down Moon smashed into it."

Jobs nodded. "I'm pretty sure it's our solar system. But where's Mars? That might be Venus over there, and that could be Saturn — you can vaguely see the rings — but Jupiter looks all wrong. It's way too bright. The whole thing, it could be our old solar system or not."

"Does Billy know about this?"

"I don't know," Jobs admitted. "He's been running Mother but he's got limits. He can't watch every subroutine. He can't keep an eye on every one of us all the time. It's enough he's maintaining all the environments. Wouldn't surprise me if that alone has him maxed out."

"I don't know how the little guy does it." Mo'Steel said with feeling.

"Billy's tougher than all of us."

"Yeah, Duck. You're right about that one."

"Let's go back," Jobs said quickly. "I've seen enough for today."

"Evaporate the illusion," Mo'Steel added.

The next moment, Jobs and Mo'Steel were stretched out on side-by-side platforms in the "attic" of the ship called Mother. Their dirty, tattered clothes had been replaced with clean T-shirts, jeans, and sneakers. Mo'Steel wore a bandanna around his head, tied in the back.

"You know it's going to cause trouble, right?" Mo'Steel asked Jobs after a while. But it was more of a rhetorical question.

Jobs nodded anyway.

"You tell the others that maybe you've found Earth, or what's left of it, and people are going to want to go check it out. And that's going to violate the Big Compromise. Very messy."

Jobs didn't respond.

"Of course," Mo'Steel went on, almost too casually, "you could always decide not to tell anyone, just keep it our little secret."

Jobs glanced at his friend but didn't respond.

"Okay," Mo'Steel said. "You obviously don't want to talk about it now. Fair enough."

He grabbed two bottles of Pepsi sitting on a small table at his side and handed one to Jobs.

Jobs unscrewed the top, took a slug, swallowed and grimaced. "I still think the flavor is off. Too sweet."

Mo'Steel grinned and looked down, examining his drink. "Well, it's a little too yellowish. Looks like pee."

"Bathroom humor?" Jobs said, trying to hide a smile.

"Yup. Right now, we need something to make us laugh. 'Cause I don't think things are gonna be too funny around here from now on."

(CHAPTER TWO)

"I'VE FOUND SOMETHING, VIOLET."

Jobs liked going to Violet's house for two reasons: Violet and the house. Of the two, Violet was the more compelling.

In the past few months since Billy had defeated the Baby/Shipwright/Maker, Jobs's relationship with Violet had deepened. He didn't know exactly if they could be considered, technically, boyfriend and girlfriend. It bothered Jobs a little, the haziness, because he liked to define things so he could understand them.

Bottom line was that Jobs and Violet liked to spend time with each other, talking mostly. It was easy and it was somehow exciting at the same time. Because some things had changed since they'd first met.

Violet no longer asked to be called Miss Blake. She was no longer officially a "Jane," though she assured Jobs she still held to certain standards of good behavior and gracious living. She no longer wore old-fashioned dresses, either, though she was still by far the most overtly feminine of the Remnants.

Violet also had a way of letting Jobs be himself. That was important considering Jobs could tell that sometimes Violet found his need to understand and explain things a bit annoying.

The house — Violet's house — was a white-washed Greek villa, complete with the kind of red-tiled roof seen throughout the Mediterranean and a veranda with low whitewashed walls and big red clay pots of lemon and olive trees. The villa sat on a rise that overlooked a tiny bright blue sea. The strength and simplicity of the colors — white, red, blue — soothed Jobs, made him feel that things were all right.

From the veranda a white-pebbled path led to a small enclosed garden, in which stood a variety of classical statues carved in white marble. Jobs even recognized a few, though he wasn't sure from where, a class trip to a museum or pictures in a textbook.

Inside the villa, Violet — with Billy's help — had created a collection of some of the world's finest paintings. Jobs recognized a few, even though he didn't necessarily know the titles or the names of the painters. There was the "Mona Lisa" by Leonardo da Vinci and, one of Jobs's favorites, "*Chiffres et Constellations,*" by a Spanish guy named Joan Miró. In all, there were more than a hundred masterpieces.

Usually, contemplating the works of art made Violet happy. Today, she was far from it.

"Art is supposed to be for private enjoyment and public consumption. But I seem to be the only one who wants to look at these paintings. Nobody comes here," Violet said. "Except you. And Noyze. I'm living by myself in a museum."

"Do you miss your mom?" Jobs asked abruptly.

"No. Yes. Sometimes."

Jobs nodded.

"But I get the feeling you didn't come over to talk about art, did you?" Violet said. "Or my mother. What's up?"

"Do you want to go outside?"

"Yeah."

They walked outside and onto the veranda, which looked out over the sparkling blue water.

"I'm pretty sure I've found something, Violet," Jobs explained. And then he began to tell her that he'd shown his discovery to Mo'Steel, and that

Mo'Steel agreed it looked an awful lot like what was left of Earth and the moon.

Violet had no discernible reaction.

"Pretty exciting, huh?" Jobs asked, somewhat weirded out by her indifference.

"I don't know what to say," she admitted. "I don't see what good it does us now to have found — Earth. Or what's left of it. It just sounds very, very sad to me. I'm sorry."

Jobs shook his head. "You don't get it, huh? There's a chance, slim but a chance, that Earth's still habitable. That we could go back and with Billy's help and the ship's resources, maybe, just maybe, the human race could be independent again. Owners and not renters. We could start over and —"

Violet began to laugh but her eyes were sad. "Oh, Jobs, you're crazy! Forget what you saw, or *think* you saw. You're only going to end up being disappointed."

Jobs ran his hand through his already unruly hair. He suddenly remembered his mother calling him Mop-Top. Back on Earth.

Back home.

He had to try to make Violet understand.

"Honestly, Violet," he said, "can you really just let this go? Don't you want to see what might be what's left of Earth, see where it takes us? Can you really just forget about it, just turn away, go on living aboard Mother for the duration? Not knowing if she'll ever decide she doesn't want us here anymore. Never knowing what might have been on Earth."

"I want to stay *here*," Violet said angrily. "It's safer. Smarter. Look, what if the planet is Earth? What then? Maybe it's not habitable. Probably it's not. What if Billy can't fix it all for us? I don't need to lose my home twice in one lifetime."

"But this is *not* home," Jobs argued.

"It is now. It is because I've chosen it to be and I've accepted its limitations. All of them. No, Jobs. I don't want to leave. I'm *not* leaving."

"You're just scared."

Violet smiled. "That's what I've been saying."

"But what if — just what if — the planet *is* Earth and it *is* habitable and we can rebuild —"

"What? Rebuild what, Jobs? A fabulous civilization, just like that? With a handful of people, some of whom are not the nicest of folks and who can't even agree on what an extra-cheese taco should taste like?"

Jobs sighed. "Just use your imagination, okay? Please?"

Violet looked at Jobs with an expression he could not decipher. Her eyes were cloudy. "Jobs, I miss home so badly," she said, her voice breaking. "I try not to think about the past but I can't help it. I dream about it almost every night. How can I try to go back to something I truly believe is no longer there?"

"But don't you ever wonder, though?" Jobs persisted. "Because maybe something good is still there. Maybe, I don't know, like trees. Maybe some people. It's probably not true, but there could be people alive there."

"People?" Violet laughed harshly and looked away. "No, Jobs. More like descendants of a few wrecked survivors of the greatest catastrophe our world has ever known. What could we possibly have in common with them? They're probably a completely different species now! They might not have a language, or machines, they might not even have the wheel for all we know! God, Jobs, they might not even be breathing oxygen! I'm saying they're not us. The human race as we know it consists of us. That's all."

"Maybe the Missing Eight are there," Jobs said, his voice nearly a whisper.

Violet just stared at him.

"Will you go along if the others choose to?" he said after a moment.

"I'm a captive to the will of the people, Jobs," Violet said. She sounded resigned. "Aren't I?"

"Aren't we all?" Jobs asked wearily.

CHAPTER THREE

"THE PAIN — IT'S STILL THERE.
BUT THE MEMORY IS FADING."

Jobs left Violet's house and went to see Mo'Steel. He found him, outside and in motion. As usual.

The house Mo'Steel shared with his mother was pretty basic. Neither was big into clutter or fancy decoration. Olga Gonzalez had chosen a spare Southwestern theme for the living room and other public parts of the one-story house.

She had a big garden with all sorts of plants and trees and flowers, from cactus plants to ferns, stuff that back on Earth would never have been able to thrive together in the same climate, under both wet and dry, bright and shady conditions. Three bonsai projects, one an already massive juniper, were in the works. Olga said gardening kept her out of trouble.

Jobs didn't quite know what she meant by that.

Mo'Steel's room was nothing more than a place to sleep a few hours each night. There was a bed, piles of clothes all over the floor — no dresser, no closet, even — various pieces of protective equipment, such as helmets, goggles, knee and elbow pads, even breast and shoulder plates. There were skates and boards and bikes. And that was pretty much it as far as Mo'Steel's room was concerned.

The thing that distinguished the Gonzalez home from the others was not actually a part of the house. It was next to and circling above and wrapping around and zooming past the house.

It was the *Mo'Run*.

The *Mo'Run* was definitely outrageous. It was like architecture by Dr. Seuss. There were tunnels and loops and slides. There was an ever-varying choice of skateboards, state-of-the-art in-line skates, bungee cords, and various forms of toboggans.

One day you could be in a cage, whipping around in a 180-degree arc. The next you could be lying on your back, strapped onto a barely-wider-than-you board, shooting down a steep, tight track at such a speed you'd be sent flying up, up to the top of the now-almost-forty-five-degree angle of the track, feet in the lead, blood rushing to your head, and — whoosh! Back the way you'd just come . . .

Or you could be in charge, testing your skills of balance and coordination and trying your nerves by tightrope walking a continually, randomly waving rail.

It was the grand-high-exalted ruler of roller coasters.

It was the ultimate in thrill-seeking pleasure. It was a supreme vision of an action park. It was Mo'Steel's masterpiece. Ever changing, ever improving, ever expanding to satisfy the need for speed, the desire for challenge.

Mo'Steel quit his warm-up routine of stretches and leaps. Sweat matted his longish brown hair and trickled down his face. Mo'Steel shook himself like a wet dog, smiled, and picked up a pair of superior Rollerblades lying on the grass.

Jobs grinned. "You do know that *Mo'Run* sounds like . . ."

"Moron? Yeah, real funny, Duck. But the name stays."

Mo'Steel finished adjusting the wheels of his blades and stretched out on the grass, hands under his head.

"Something on your mind?"

"How could you tell?" Jobs said wryly.

"Just a hunch," Mo'Steel grinned.

Jobs sat down next to his friend and told him about Violet's reaction to his big news. Mo'Steel wasn't surprised.

"You know how I feel," he said. "Kind of like Violet, like things are good enough now, let's just work on making them better. Also, I kind of feel like you do. Like, let's take the big chance, start out new on our own planet. I don't know. I guess I'll just wait and see where the majority vote lands and do what I have to do."

"We're not officially a democracy," Jobs remarked. "But I know what you mean. If the ship goes, we go. Free will has its limits here."

Mo'Steel grinned. "It always does, Duck, always did, even back on good ole Earth."

Mo'Steel jumped up. Jobs followed him to the shed that housed a bunch of spare parts for the *Mo'Run*.

"Anyway, I've been wanting to say I'm glad you and Violet are, you know, hanging out."

"Yeah. Thanks."

Mo'Steel cleared his throat nervously. "I won't ask if you ever think about Cordelia, because I know you do. But — does it get any better?"

Jobs thought about that. "I don't know," he admitted. "The pain — it's still there. But the memory is fading. It's just not all as vivid as it was."

"That's good."

"Is it? It hasn't been that long since . . ."

"Yeah, since the world fell apart. For us it hasn't been that long, Jobs. For them, they've been gone five hundred years. That's a lot of years."

Jobs smiled ruefully. "I don't know why I always found this funny but . . . my uncle used to say to me, 'Jobs, have fun while you can because you're dead a long time.' "

"He was so right," Mo'Steel said.

"What about you, Mo'? Is there anyone . . . ?"

Mo'Steel laughed. "What do you think?"

"There's Tate. She seems nice."

Mo'Steel raised his eyebrows. "Yeah. She's really cool. But I just don't think she's interested in me that way."

"You think she likes guys more, I don't know, into computers and stuff?"

Mo'Steel shrugged. "I don't know. Just — there's no one. Noyze is a sweet kid but she's a kid. 2Face's personality is just scary. Ditto Tamara, even though that's not her fault. Dr. Cohen is old enough to be my mother. And my mother *is* my mother, so . . ."

"I see what you mean." Jobs felt bad for bringing up the subject.

"If this were a real utopia," Mo'Steel said, brightening, "I'd be hanging with —"

"Utopias aren't real," Jobs said cutting Mo'Steel off. It was what bothered him about life on Mother. "They're impossible."

"I'm just saying that if . . . never mind. I'm just saying that I'm happy for you and Violet and all, but sometimes, man, it'd be nice to have a femme to hang with, you know?"

"Yeah. I guess the cartoons Billy summons up don't really count, huh? Like that red-haired clerk at Foot Locker."

"Yeah. Something about the two-dimensional thing is kinda weird. I don't know."

Mo'Steel focused on choosing and buckling on protective equipment.

Jobs and Mo'Steel could joke about the flaws and idiosyncracies of the world they'd created for themselves out of memory, desire, and imagination. But behind the fancy houses and the new clothes there was an emptiness that no amount of computer-generated stuff could fill.

No doubt about it, The Zone — the Remnants'

environment — was a strange and sometimes uncomfortable mix of the fantastic and the mundane.

A river wound through The Zone, sometimes raging and whitecapped, sometimes placid and slow, with no relation at all to the weather or the terrain. Verdant hills rose abruptly from desert plains, which bordered improbably on lush coniferous forests. The landscape of The Zone was a weird patchwork of scenes, with a few signs of logical compromise and more signs of individualism and selfishness.

Like Yago's castle.

Jobs thought of the famous cliché: Beauty is in the eye of the beholder. And he wasn't beholding any beauty in Yago's increasingly larger structure. Every time Yago added a turret or a tower, Jobs's view of the sunset was further blocked. He'd asked Yago — through his lackey, D-Caf — for a compromise, but Yago wasn't having any of it.

At any rate, Jobs and Edward's house was pretty straightforward. It was divided into two sections, one for each brother. For Jobs, there was the lab of his dreams, where he tried to research a variety of topics that interested him.

Jobs was most interested in the notion of the existential computer, something that would be considered an inseparable, integral part of the person wearing it.

Other topics interested Jobs, too, topics that related in some way to his quest for a habitable planet. Like the life cycle of star systems.

And dinosaurs. Like the human race, they had been victims of a global catastrophe. Some scientists had thought their extinction was caused by a massive meteorite hitting Earth. Jobs wondered if some species had lingered on for millennia after the destruction of the world as they'd known it. Could that be true, too, for humans? As crazy as it sounded, maybe there *had* been some survivors of the Rock. . . .

Jobs's bedroom was, by contrast, simple, basically a bed, a desk, and a chair. He'd chosen a blue for the walls and ceiling, a color as close as he could remember to the color of the Pacific Ocean on that day when he'd taken out the Ford Libertad! And driven along the coast and discovered that the world was coming to an end.

Edward's bedroom was a kid's fantasy playroom. There was an entire playground, complete with sandbox, jungle gym, and superslide. There were banks of computer games and old-fashioned pinball machines. There were piles of Frisbees and beach balls and softball equipment. There was an amazing Erector set, bikes, scooters, and even though there was no snow, there was a Flexible Flyer, just in case Edward's petition for a few wintry days was granted. His bed was in the shape of a race car and the sheets were printed with superheroes.

Edward was Jobs's little brother, only six years old — give or take five hundred years — and Jobs still felt the responsibility of any older brother. But in some ways Edward was way beyond Jobs in experience.

He was now the Chameleon, thanks to a mutation that had occurred at some time during the *Mayflower*'s long journey. He could blend into his surroundings in a very disconcerting way. He could be seen and not seen. He could use the habits of the human eye to his advantage.

Lately, Edward had taken to leaving the house and not returning for hours on end. When Jobs asked him where he'd been, Edward always gave the same answer. "Searching for clues."

It worried Jobs not to know where Edward was at all times. He felt he owed it to the memory of their parents to keep his little brother safe from harm. But the reality was that Jobs couldn't keep Edward under constant surveillance. Not when Edward himself had become a master spy.

"Uh, Jobs?"

Jobs looked up, startled. "Sorry. Just thinking."

Mo'Steel laughed. "Something you do too much of, 'migo, to the detriment of your physical health. Sure you don't want to try the *Mo'Run?*"

"How is riding that fifteen-story death trap good for my health? But — okay."

(CHAPTER FOUR)

"MAYBE WE SHOULD GET OUT OF HERE WHILE WE CAN."

Jobs's visit had gotten to Violet. Maybe it was just one of those gloomy days, the kind given to dark thoughts and bad memories. But she didn't think so.

Now Violet was restless. Her mind wouldn't stop, and her skin felt all twitchy. She walked through room after room of great art and comfortable furniture and saw none of it.

She thought about how in the beginning, everyone had been eager to show off his or her house. There'd been a flurry of visits, a fair amount of bragging, compliments thrown around. And then, it had all stopped. As if by agreement everyone had retreated into his or her private mini-world, his or her personal kingdom, and shut the door.

Still, it bothered her, this self-imposed isolation

everyone had grabbed. It meant a lack of real community. And a lack of real concern for one another.

The town center, for example, was a joke. It was there because everyone remembered their hometown or city having a central place of business and social activity. So it had seemed necessary to construct one here.

Violet stopped her nervous pacing, sat down on the edge of a Louis XIV chair, and stared into space. The silence was huge.

Not everyone lived alone. Violet had chosen to because who would she have chosen as a housemate? Noyze had Dr. Cohen, a friend and sort of surrogate mother. They kept each other good company. Mo'Steel lived with his mother, another logical choice.

Jobs had Edward. Yago, his toadies, D-Caf and Anamull. Tamara no longer had her baby — the Baby — which was both a blessing and a cruelty. But now she had Tate, who seemed to have appointed herself Tamara's guardian. And Tate had also taken in Roger Dodger, for whom she acted as a protective big sister.

That left T.R. in his nondescript split-level ranch house. Violet smiled when she thought of it. For a psychiatrist, T.R. did not display a lot of imagination.

Burroway also lived solo — except for the so-called company of cartoon "help" — in a pseudo-English cottage. Actually, it seemed to Violet more of a mini–manor house. Very appropriate for someone with delusions of grandeur.

2Face lived alone and that seemed natural. Violet couldn't imagine such an independent person sharing space with anyone. Kubrick, too, had his own place. It pained Violet to acknowledge that the poor boy was probably better off living alone than with someone who was struggling to pretend that Kubrick, with his see-through skin, didn't gross them out.

Violet sighed, stood, and stretched. "Maybe Jobs is right," she said out loud. "Maybe we should get out of here while we can."

"What are you doing here?"

Kubrick flinched. So much for "Hi. How are you?" Instead he said, "I know you're busy. . . ."

"Come in." 2Face turned away from the door and walked inside. Kubrick hesitated, then followed, closing the door behind him.

2Face's house was a disturbing place. The pool was okay, though Kubrick had never been much of a swimmer. 2Face had told him straight out that the water was unchlorinated because chlorine still stung her scars.

That was the thing about the house, and about 2Face. They were both so in-your-face, so about the fire that had transformed beautiful Essence Hwang into a girl with a grudge. It both attracted and repelled Kubrick.

Like the way 2Face had decorated every single wall with mirrors, even in the kitchen. Like she couldn't stop looking at herself, reminding herself of who she was. Or maybe it was that she *wouldn't* stop looking. Kubrick wasn't sure he wanted to know either way.

Besides, it wasn't like his own place didn't say something about who he had become. Maybe who he'd always been — a freak. A failed experiment of his father's. And of Mother. The difference between his house and 2Face's was that hers seemed somehow a fierce celebration of who she was, while his was definitely not.

Kubrick had *no* mirrors, on the walls or anywhere else. He still couldn't bear to look at himself and was pretty sure he never would be able to stand the sight. He saw the way people's eyes darted away. But 2Face was the one who *never* flinched.

So visiting her was tough because Kubrick had to keep his eyes on her, or keep them closed. Too many mirrors.

"Are you ashamed of yourself?" she'd demanded once, angrily.

"Yeah." He'd told her the truth.

Now that he could choose his own clothing, he chose long-sleeved shirts, turtlenecks, long pants, gloves, a baseball cap, sometimes with a bandanna underneath. Unlike Mo'Steel's, Kubrick's bandanna wasn't about attitude or mopping up sweat. It was about coverage. He'd even considered wrapping up his face. But he hadn't gone that far. Yet.

Kubrick followed 2Face into the kitchen. He watched as she took bread from the bread box, ham from the refrigerator, tomatoes from a bowl on the counter. He watched as, seemingly ignoring him, she began to make sandwiches.

Kubrick tugged at his gloves, though they were as far up over his skinless wrists as they could go.

"Do you think the Baby is really gone?" he said. "The Shipwright, I mean."

"You came over to ask me that?" 2Face sighed dramatically and put down the knife she was using to slice the bread. "Kubrick, I have no idea what really happened to that — whatever *it* was — and I don't really care. As long as Billy stays where he is and does what we ask him."

"I was wondering," Kubrick blurted. "Do you

think Billy could, you know, maybe change me back to normal?"

2Face gave Kubrick a challenging look. "Why would you want to do that?" she said.

To himself Kubrick answered, *So you would go out with me. So people wouldn't want to throw up when they see me.*

But he couldn't say those things aloud, to anyone, least of all to 2Face.

So he said nothing.

"You think you're all vulnerable, everything showing, nothing hidden, don't you?" she asked.

Kubrick didn't answer her. He felt tears coming to his eyes and tried to blink them back but there was nothing to blink them back with. Why had he come?

"Like you're the walking wounded, a big gaping hole everyone can see into, a . . ."

"Stop," Kubrick said.

"A freak." 2Face stared at him. Her eyes were hard. Kubrick couldn't understand why she hated him so much.

He turned to leave.

"That's too bad," he heard her say, her voice louder, catching him. Kubrick stopped. "Because you're really just like everyone else. Want some lunch?"

CHAPTER FIVE

D-CAF WANTED VERY BADLY TO GO HOME.

Yago had dragged them out here, to the edge of The Zone, again. D-Caf guessed they were probably going to meet another Blue Meanie. He was supposed to keep quiet about these meetings, and so far he had. But sometimes the urge to tell someone about what Yago was up to was so strong. Not that D-Caf really understood exactly what Yago was doing, but he knew enough to know Yago was probably causing trouble for the others.

The east edge of The Zone was a very pretty forested area, re-created from famous paintings and beautiful photographs. D-Caf liked it here. It was deep green and peaceful and the air smelled fresh and piney. It made D-Caf happy, even though just beyond the forest, smack up against it like a line had been drawn, no transition, was the Riders' environment. That swampy place, with the copper-colored water and the goofy trembling trees. That, D-Caf could do without, but it was part of the Big Compromise that Billy maintain the Riders' environment.

"Dude," Anamull said, pointing to the sky, "here comes one now."

D-Caf looked furtively at Yago. His face bore that weird "I am seeing more than what you all see" expression. And why did he always have to wear white clothes? White shirt, white pants, even white shoes.

A single Blue Meanie came in for a landing. From a distance D-Caf could never tell one Meanie from another. But up close, even though their blue-black suits were identical and didn't even allow their eyes to be seen, somehow D-Caf could immediately recognize individuality. Yago found this ability of D-Caf's useful.

The Blue Meanie got closer. It was wearing his blue-black armor, of course, that doubled as a flying suit. The suit/armor covered every inch of the Meanie's body. But D-Caf knew what this Meanie really looked like.

Its body was kind of pony-shaped and pony-sized. It had four legs that tapered into feet that weren't really feet. The Meanie was hairless. No fur, either. Its skin was rubbery and wrinkly. Its head was low-slung and its eyes, intelligent. On either side of its head was a snaky tentacle. D-Caf had seen the Meanies use their tentacles to communicate in a sort of sign language, as well as to perform tasks. The tentacles were like human hands in that way.

The Blue Meanie landed. His name was Three Glowing Moons. They had met with this Meanie before. He was one of Yago's favorites. No matter how often Yago repeated his crazy message, Three Glowing Moons seemed willing to listen.

Yago wasted no time getting started.

"It is good that you are here," Yago intoned. "There is no time to waste. The Mother you once knew and loved has fallen. Mother is no more, but in her place has arisen another even more worthy of your respect. That person is me. I am Yago."

D-Caf had heard it all before. Yago was the one who was followed by the Few. The Few were the Chosen. The Freaks and their protectors were not among the Chosen. Blah blah blah.

"Mother is weak," Yago went on. "She allowed herself to be taken over by an outsider, an alien to the Children's true cause. That alien is the human called Billy. How can she continue to be your guiding light when she herself is so blind?"

Another Blue Meanie was coming in slowly for a landing. When it was on the ground it approached

Three Glowing Moons and Yago cautiously. D-Caf was sure he'd never seen this Meanie before.

Yago never missed a beat. "You will henceforth be known as the ones who follow Yago. You will change your names from those celebrating Mother to those celebrating me."

"The Grand Mystic Poo-Bah." D-Caf giggled.

Anamull snorted. "Hey. Nice to meet you. My name is Yago's Big Butt."

"I'm Yago's . . ."

Anamull shoved him before he could finish his sentence.

"Ow!"

Yago turned and glared at D-Caf with his golden catlike eyes. D-Caf looked down at his feet.

D-Caf knew he had to be careful what he said around Yago. Yago was becoming more and more unpredictable. His anger was getting more and more out of control. D-Caf was pretty sure that Yago was sick. In the head.

But sometimes Yago was just so funny. He didn't mean to be but he was. And D-Caf couldn't help but laugh.

Still, D-Caf was grateful to Yago for being the only one of the Wakers to talk to him from the start, to treat him like a person. Even though D-Caf knew that from the beginning Yago was using him, that he probably didn't even like him. But at least Yago acknowledged his existence, found something for him to do at every turn, and when you're all alone, alone like no one else in the world has ever quite been, you'll take any form of friendship you can get.

Like that girl Tate, the one with the shaved head except for a bunch of dreadlocks at the back gathered into a ponytail that hung halfway down her back. She had trusted him when she and Roger Dodger had been escaping from the Riders. D-Caf smiled at the thought. Riding those hoverboards had been very cool. He'd been very good at it, too. He'd felt proud and that was a very new feeling for D-Caf.

He never felt anything but stupid around Yago, even when Yago was being odd.

But when it had come time to actually settle down and live somewhere, D-Caf had chosen to live with Yago. Well, actually, Yago had told D-Caf and Anamull that they would be staying with him. But D-Caf hadn't protested. He knew he'd basically be Yago's servant, but that was better than being alone with no one to talk to. Or to listen to.

And Yago could be entertaining. As well as creepy. Lately, he'd taken to muttering about Billy being his archrival. Stuff that made D-Caf think that Yago was seriously looney.

Nevertheless, D-Caf lived with Yago and Anamull in what was called the Castle. It was grandiose beyond anything D-Caf had ever seen back on Earth. It was all white marble and purple velvet and gold stuff, like candelabra and picture frames, even the crown that Yago wore every night at dinner. There were at least fifty rooms at any given time. D-Caf had given up counting or keeping track of them because Yago was always petitioning Billy for changes. Even now D-Caf sometimes got lost in the ever-changing labyrinth that was the second floor.

D-Caf and Anamull each had his own bedroom — Yago wasn't stingy, at least — and Yago had a personal suite of rooms that included a bathroom the size of D-Caf's old house back on Earth. On the first floor there was a throne room where Yago spent several hours each day being waited upon by a corps of cartoons in fancy costumes. D-Caf had learned that the costumes were an amalgamation of styles from classical Rome and ancient Egypt.

The overall architecture and style of the Castle also combined elements from these two cultures, like walls painted with scenes of people feasting, and golden sphinxes, as well as lots of rich trappings, like bronze spiraled columns and elaborate stained-glass windows from the Italian Renaissance. Violet had pointed out stuff taken almost directly from St. Peter's Basilica in Rome.

D-Caf didn't think Violet liked him, but she was polite to him, and that mattered a lot.

Outside, the Castle was all white because Yago said white was pure. That was one of his favorite words: pure.

The roof of the Castle was decorated with a never-ending succession of turrets and towers and spirals and glittering silver triangular shapes and a big gold ball with nine little gold balls circling it. Yago kept D-Caf and Anamull busy delivering requests to Billy for more *stuff* to be put up there. If anyone had asked him, D-Caf would have said there was more than enough big ugly stuff up there already. But nobody asked him, so he kept his mouth shut.

D-Caf came back to the present just in time for the weird thing Yago always did to the Meanies who came to see him.

Three Glowing Moons beckoned to his recently arrived companion.

"Are you ready to receive the gift of touch?" Yago intoned.

Anamull took a step back. D-Caf thought that was a good idea. He stepped back, too, landed on Anamull's foot, got a slap in the back of the head.

With Three Glowing Moons helping him, the second Meanie removed one of his tentacles from the blue-black suit.

Looks like a big wrinkly worm, D-Caf thought.

Three Glowing Moons pushed the second Meanie forward so that he stood close to Yago. Then Yago reached out and placed his bare hand on the Meanie's tentacle.

D-Caf didn't know what was happening, though he'd seen Yago do this before.

And it was the same every time. The second Meanie was sent into a deep well of emotion. D-Caf didn't know exactly what the Meanie was feeling but he knew it was powerful. His armored body shook.

When Yago removed his hand, the Meanie collapsed against Three Glowing Moons.

Maybe Yago really has something powerful going on, D-Caf thought uneasily. *Or maybe, like Edward, the chameleon kid, Yago had been mutated by five hundred years of exposure to radiation. Or maybe . . . maybe any human could touch a Meanie on his bare flesh and the Meanie would react.*

D-Caf didn't know the answer and had a feeling that if he asked Yago, he'd get only some mumbo jumbo. And he didn't feel comfortable asking Anamull.

The second Meanie had covered his tentacle once again with his suit.

Yago spoke. "Now go and deliver my message to your people," he said. "Tell them I can show them the way to perfect happiness."

When Three Glowing Moons' companion had recovered his senses, Three Glowing Moons withdrew something from a pouch slung across his chest, bandolier style, and handed it to Yago. Across the screen on his chest scrolled the words: *Accept my gift.*

It was a small fléchette gun, the kind D-Caf had seen too many times before. This particular weapon, usually part of the Meanies' armor, had been fitted out with a handle built for a human hand. It had been made especially for Yago.

The delight on Yago's face was unmistakable. He was like a little kid with a new toy. In one swift, graceful movement, Yago swung around, took aim at a huge old oak tree, and fired.

D-Caf squeezed his eyes shut against the sound.

After a moment, he opened them. The tree had been ripped apart, branches severed, its trunk now a stack of slivers.

Yago held the fléchette gun to his chest. "It will do," he mumbled. "It will do."

At that moment, D-Caf wanted very badly to go home.

CHAPTER SIX

BILLY WEIR WAS SO ALONE.

Billy Weir reclined in one of the chairs that allowed him to interface with the computers.

He was the master programmer. He hadn't exactly asked for that role. He didn't really have a choice about defeating the Baby, the Maker, the Shipwright named Te. Could he have chosen not to incorporate Mother?

Billy had a lot to think about.

Sometimes he now saw himself and the world around him as if through the multilensed eyes of a fly, a hundred tiny reclining chairs, a thousand tiny computers, a million tiny Billys. He saw every image at once, though distinctly, like watching a wall of TV screens, each showing a different image, but each image somehow part of a whole, of one master image.

Billy knew it shouldn't make sense, but to him, it did.

The experience was more like looking through a kaleidoscope, everything and everyone bright and fragmented, shifting, forming one big design, then flowering into another, in a rhythmic dance that spoke nothing but truth.

Billy knew he was alone in the way he saw things. Always had been.

He saw things that were in his field of sight. He saw things that were far, far away. Vision and per-spective were interesting matters.

Billy rarely ventured out into The Zone he'd cre-ated for the others. He spent most of his time in a tiny, spare room just off the bridge, or on the bridge itself. The bridge was a massive space, octagonal in shape. Computer equipment, originally designed for the Shipwrights, was everywhere. The ceiling was a giant screen that revealed the space through which the ship traveled.

When Billy had first reached the bridge, the computers had been littered with odds and ends. It seemed the Shipwrights had long since ceased to actively control the ship; Mother had been set on autopilot and the bridge was used mainly as a sort of library or meeting room. When Billy took over, he'd gotten rid of the Shipwrights' *tchotchkes*. He'd left the simple geometric designs, mere decoration, where they were.

Billy wasn't interested in much these days. He wasn't even interested in food anymore, though the truth was that he'd never been much interested in food. That was something his father, Big Bill, had just not understood. Billy ate simple foods now, simply to keep his body alive, his heart pumping blood through his veins.

And Billy kept his body alive because the others relied on him. Because if he was no longer, their safety in The Zone would be no longer. And he felt he owed them — some of them, anyway — for taking care of him when he'd slowed so far down it was as if he didn't exist.

Billy wanted to stay as he was now because he knew something was happening to him. Again.

Billy had the strong sense that he was becoming less human and more something — else. And he was curious to learn what, exactly, he was becoming.

Because Billy was pretty sure that what he was becoming — maybe what he had already become — was not part of the human race's past or its future. This disturbed him. And it excited him.

Billy couldn't forget. Just before the Baby/Ship-wright/Maker had died — just after Billy had absorbed Mother into his own self — the Maker had said to Billy: "*You* are not human."

"I'm human," Billy had asserted, but even then he hadn't been sure of this. There had been doubt, occasioned by a vague memory of shapes, pulsating energy fields . . . something. The vagueness of the memory had disturbed Billy more than anything, used as he was to amazingly vivid recall even of memories not his own.

He'd told himself the memory was just a remembered hallucination.

What else had the dying Maker said? Yes: "The ancient enemy." The remark was cryptic then and remained a mystery. Was Billy that ancient enemy? The ancient enemy of whom?

The one thing Billy *was* interested in was himself.

"I need to know," he whispered to the empty room.

What potential did he possess, for good, for evil? What was his purpose, why was he here? Or was his life just a random series of cosmic accidents and grand mistakes?

Had he, alone among all other humans, suffered

a cataclysmic evolution, an almost instantaneous transformation, somewhere along the line in his life?

Was he forever separated from the human race? Had he always been? Could he ever go back and if he could, if he even wanted to, who would show him the way?

Billy Weir was so alone.

Okay. So the time had come. He would go back to the start and follow the path to the future. He would find himself along the way.

He hoped.

He closed his eyes. It began immediately.

The appearance of life on Earth. Three-point-six to three-point-seven billion years before Earth's destruction by the Rock.

All life descending from a primordial protoplasmic mass, all life originating in the sea.

Billy focused. He experienced himself from the simplest component, the most basic building block of all life.

Billy knew himself as a strand of DNA. The structure that every schoolkid knew encoded the essence of a species. The thing that all living things had in common — genetics.

Too rapidly for true evolutionary process, Billy

watched himself expand into a simple one-celled animal, an amoeba.

Billy hurried through the next phases of devel-
opment. Like time-lapse photography times one
hundred, Billy grew. Others grew with him. Now he
was a small mammal scurrying under the trunklike
legs of a herbivorous dinosaur, one of the bron-
tosaurus variety.

Billy looked and listened. Along the evolutionary
path, instinct was joined by critical thought. Language began to develop, signs and sounds, eventually
speech and writing and so, art. Prehistory became
history.

The wheel was invented and light shone from
the dark. Economics was born. Hunters and gather-
ers became farmers and then there were towns and
then cities. The notions of leisure and luxury took
hold, as did the notion of master and servant.

Human beings struggled, fought, loved, and nur-
tured. They developed new emotions like shame
and new concepts like sin. They domesticated other
species. They made government.

But nothing in the long evolution of man explained Billy. Nothing revealed a clue as to what Billy
had become and why. He extended the sequence

into the future. The future that might now never come.

Now the human animal was no longer recognizable as the upright, two-legged creature it had been in the year 2011, when the Rock had destroyed planet Earth. In Billy's mind the human that was Billy and every other human rapidly became a sleek, hairless, translucent creature with a sea of tiny antennae rising from its scalp.

Nothing.

Billy stopped the process. Nothing in the long sequence of human evolution explained him. Nothing.

What Billy had become was not a part of the human past or a part of its future. Billy was a wild trajectory off the evolutionary path.

Billy Weir was alone.

CHAPTER SEVEN

"THERE'S A PLACE I CAN'T GO."

Jobs had mixed feelings about visiting Billy on the bridge or in his small room. He didn't like to bother Billy while he was working, which was always. But he felt a sort of companionship with Billy. And a sense of being Billy's big brother somehow, protector of a genius kid the other kids picked on.

But, right now, Billy was pretty much in charge, wasn't he? He'd defeated the Baby/Shipwright/Maker and taken over Mother.

Jobs had known from the beginning that Billy was special, different, strong, and had wanted so badly to know what that specialness meant, what it could do, what Billy could achieve. Partly it was Jobs's insatiable curiosity that had driven him to care for Billy in his comatose state; partly, it was Jobs's highly developed sense of morality, social responsibility, feelings about what one person owed to another.

He found Billy reclining in his usual interface chair, the place from which he basically ran the ship now that Mother was — gone. Jobs knew that Billy saw him but that at the same time Billy saw other things, too, the Remnants, the Riders and Meanies, far parts of the ship, everything all at once. Jobs was only one screen among the thousands in Billy's consciousness.

Billy didn't waste time on a greeting.

"Tell me about what you've found," he said.

"You know?"

Billy didn't answer. Jobs wondered if Billy had been watching his journey through space, or if he just sensed Jobs had some news?

"Well," Jobs's voice cracked as he spoke.

Jobs told Billy what he — and then Mo'Steel — had seen, and where. There was no way for him to read Billy's reaction to the information. Emotions never showed on his face. His body never twitched or shifted or shook to indicate feelings. Though he seemed to be looking at Jobs, Jobs had the feeling Billy was also looking at something else far, far away.

"In general," Billy asked, "who are the ones who want to stay where they are and perfect The Zone?"

"Violet," Jobs said. "I told her what I found. She

wasn't impressed. Olga. Dr. Cohen and Noyze. Kubrick. And Burroway."

"They're content?"

"They've said so in the past. They know things aren't perfect, they know it's all computer-generated and not real, but they're willing to accept it. I think they feel sort of safe."

Billy was silent for a moment. Then: "What do the others want?"

"Some want to get aggressive," Jobs said. "They want to spread beyond the one node we have, destroy the Blue Meanie threat, and take over the ship completely."

"They want to ignore the Big Compromise. Who are they? Besides Yago."

"Yes. Though he's been acting so strangely, I can't get a reading on what he really wants. Anamull and D-Caf, of course. They'll do just about anything he says. And I've heard T.R. say taking over the ship sounds like a good idea. But I don't really know how he'd vote if push comes to shove."

"Who else?"

"I'm pretty sure 2Face is an expansionist, too," Jobs told him. "She's always saying how the situation we've created is unstable at best. 2Face isn't the kind of person to sit still for long."

"She has plans?" Billy said.

Jobs shrugged. "Probably."

"Is that it?"

"No. I'm pretty sure Tamara is with them. I don't know why. And Tate. I don't know what Roger Dodger thinks. He's just a kid and he doesn't say much but he lives with Tamara and Tate so . . ."

"Edward lives with you," Billy pointed out. "He's your brother. And since the Big Compromise you've said that what you want most is to find a habitable planet and colonize it. So, how does Edward vote?"

"He's too little to really understand the options. But I don't know." Jobs frowned. "He sticks by me, sure. But he also really likes 2Face. Remember, she saved his life. She's a sort of hero to him."

"That leaves Mo'Steel."

"And you, Billy."

"That leaves Mo'Steel," Billy repeated. "He's your best friend."

"But he's got a mom. I think he's confused. But he doesn't talk much about it. Or about what *he* wants." Jobs grinned. "Except for a girlfriend."

"So, what do you think?" Billy asked. "You think people will change their minds about staying on board Mother when they hear what you've found?"

"I think it's a good bet some of the others will want to turn the ship around and head for the planet."

For the first time since Jobs had entered the room, Billy looked directly at him.

"You mean, *you* want to turn the ship around."

Jobs nodded. "Yes. But I know what the risks are. I know what could happen."

"Do you?"

"It would take generations to get there, for one."

"No. Less time than that."

"How much less?" Jobs was intrigued.

"I'll show you," Billy said.

And then Jobs was swept out of the attic, off the bridge, and into . . . into a vision of numbers, clear and precise, a vision of equations, of truths . . . a vision of stars and of space, and past, present, and future in one lovely, swirling, twisting strand, binding him, freeing him . . . And then the numbers again, coming faster and larger and closer . . . Jobs was on his back, his stomach, his feet, his head, he felt wonderful, he was in pain, it was so beautiful and true and it was too much, too much. . . .

He heard himself cry out and all the numbers went away and all that was left was the beautiful swirling strand and then . . . all of space, a wavy surface, curved and rippled and twisted and . . . Mother, Mother poking a perfect hole right though the waving surface of space and time and . . .

Jobs sat down hard on his butt. "Oh. Okay. Wormholes. Mother can tunnel through time and space."

"Six months, if everything goes okay." Billy said. "But we can be sure the Children won't be happy. We'll be going against the Big Compromise by changing the ship's course. Remember?"

Jobs shook his head. "Yeah. The deal is we can look for a habitable planet within reach of Mother's present course. When — if — we find a planet we promised to leave Mother and turn over control to the Meanies."

"And if more than a small course change is needed to reach the planet," Billy added, "we've promised to ask for the Meanies' permission before going ahead. I'll turn Mother around almost 180 degrees. I don't think the Meanies will go for that. They've made it clear they have their own agenda. So we'd have to do this on our own. We have to break the rules of the Big Compromise."

Jobs felt distinctly uncomfortable hearing the naked truth spoken aloud. But he also knew exactly what he wanted.

"They'll fight us," Jobs responded. "Can we fight back?"

"You mean, can *I* fight for all of us?" Billy asked and closed his eyes. "I'm still limited by Mother's fail-safe subroutines, Jobs. You know that. In battle I might not be much help at all."

"Okay. Okay. But if the others vote to turn Mother around . . ."

"So you're going to tell them what you think you've found?"

"Yes. Do I have a choice? So, will you help us?"

Billy opened his eyes and sat up in the chair.

"Do *I* have a choice?" he asked quietly. "If I turn Mother around I want you to do something for me."

"Okay," Jobs said warily.

"There's a place I can't go," Billy said. "One place in Mother I'm locked out of. A dark place."

Jobs nodded. Billy was starting to really freak him out.

"Go there for me, Jobs." Billy's tone was pretty urgent. "And then come back and tell me what's there."

"What do you think I'm going to find?" Jobs said. "You have any idea?"

"I think you'll find the answer."

(CHAPTER EIGHT)

"HERE WE GO, KIDDIES."

They met in the town center, at the old-fashioned whitewashed bandstand on the grassy square. No one had requested a town hall be generated, so none had been.

There was no hospital, either. Dr. Cohen had opened a medical office but so far, no one had really gotten sick.

There had been a restaurant for a while but no one seemed to know a lot about gourmet food. So after a two-thirds majority vote — Billy's rule for any changes to the shared, public areas — that was gone now. There was a fast-food place that combined decor and other elements from McDonald's, Burger King, KFC, Taco Bell, and Disney World. There was a Mexican place that repeated the Taco Bell selections and added the more popular dishes, like extra-large nachos and chicken quesadillas, from ChiChi's.

Some of the Remnants had asked for several clothing and shoe stores. As they didn't actually have to pay for the merchandise, these stores seemed to be always full of cartoon "customers" and almost always out of stock. On one occasion, Olga Gonzalez had been seen carrying home no fewer than seven shopping bags.

There was a sporting goods store, which, at Tamara's request, supported a public gym on the second floor, boasting state-of-the-art exercise equipment. State-of-the-art equipment that back in the year 2011, five hundred years in the past, every professional body builder would have killed for.

So far, no one but Tamara had used the facility.

There was no public library and no movie theater. A Starbucks and a Publix grocery store completed the town center.

People got from one place to another mostly by walking. In the beginning there had been a few cars. Jobs had requested one, as had 2Face and Burroway. But driving had proved an awkward and inefficient method of transportation as there were no public roads, no transit authority to set standards and establish rules and regulations. With so many voices and so many individual desires, a well-maintained public road was an impossibility. Roads stopped or started abruptly and were apt to change on an almost daily basis as Billy received and filtered and executed requests for pretty hillocks or gravel paths or romantic roads to nowhere.

Maybe the most ridiculous of the attempts at an individual statement had been T.R.'s personal helicopter. Aside from the fact that he had no idea how to pilot the copter — though Billy easily could have created an autopilot program — there was no place for T.R. to pilot the copter *to*. An afternoon jaunt to Rider territory? Blue Meanie—ville? The center of town, to have a one-sided chat with the two-dimensional pedestrians Billy had created to lend reality to the place?

The helicopter sat unused on T.R.'s suburban lawn, an uncomfortable reminder to some — like Jobs — of the ultimate folly of their life aboard Mother.

"Thanks for coming, everyone," Jobs said loudly. Voices dropped to murmurs, then whispers, then silence as Jobs stood waiting. The "sun" was shining and a gentle "breeze" blew wisps of hair into Jobs's eyes.

"What's up?" 2Face asked.

Jobs told them. He told them about the solar system he had found and about the lumpy planet he thought might be the remains of Earth and the moon. He explained to them about its being at the very limits of Mother's sensors, thus requiring the ship to change course by 180 degrees, should they want to go there. He reminded them that to do so would be in violation of the Big Compromise. He told them how long the trip would take. . . .

Dr. Cohen put her hand to her chest. "Eighty years? We'll be dead by then!" They were the first words anyone had said since Jobs had begun to speak.

"But our children might not be," T.R. said. "And our grandchildren."

"Oh, right," 2Face said. "Our little mutations, you mean."

Tamara flinched. Tate patted her back.

"Why would anyone want to bring a child into this . . . this place? Bad enough we're here."

Dr. Cohen nodded. "I'm with Olga."

"Everybody! Listen. It won't actually take eighty years. Mother has the ability to tunnel through space," Jobs explained.

"What does that mean?" Noyze asked.

"Think wormholes," Jobs said. "Portals between different parts of the universe, linked by black holes."

Noyze looked blank. She wasn't the only one.

"Like, warp speed on *Star Trek?*" Roger Dodger said. "My father used to watch the repeats of that show."

Jobs sighed.

"Look," he said, "it would take too long for me to explain the whole thing. Just trust me on this. Billy told me that, in theory, Mother could get us to the planet in six months. The timing is not the problem."

"The Blue Meanies are the problem," 2Face said.

"*Exactly*," Jobs said. "They've got some agenda we know nothing about. They don't want us to alter Mother's course in any major way. And we promised we wouldn't. Now we're considering breaking that promise."

"For our own needs," Violet muttered.

"What else?" 2Face.

"Jobs," Olga said, "what does Billy think of this?"

"He . . ." Jobs shrugged. "I think he'll do what we ask him. Even if he has reservations. But he does want something in exchange."

Mo'Steel grinned his wild grin. "Here we go, kiddies."

CHAPTER NINE

"I'D LIKE TO BE SPECIAL."

The Blue Meanies were camped out just beyond the east, forested edge of The Zone. Edward didn't know where exactly they had lived a long time ago when their ancestors had been created to take care of Mother. All he knew was that since the Big Compromise they'd asked to be left alone in the environment Billy created for them.

Edward didn't understand the Meanies' environment. There were long, simple structures made of what looked like the same dark shiny stuff their armor was made of. They reminded Edward of army barracks.

Maybe only the soldiers lived there. Anyway, Edward didn't have the guts to sneak inside one of the buildings so he didn't know what really went on. Maybe the Meanies had secret labs, like Jobs's, where they were developing new and better weapons to fight the humans.

Edward was sure they were up to something bad.

Aside from the barracks there were no other buildings. The ground was something like pressed sand. And there were no trees and stuff.

Edward had come here a lot lately. He'd been to lots of places he shouldn't have, like Yago's Castle and the Riders' swampy home, and no one had ever known. Edward liked to find things out for himself. People, like his big brother, considered him just a kid and nobody told a kid anything.

But Edward was more than just a kid. He was the Chameleon. He wasn't invincible but he definitely had superpowers. 2Face had told him so.

And lately he'd figured that maybe he could use those superpowers to fight the bad guys. Because if he could secretly watch on the Blue Meanies and the Riders and Yago — who 2Face said was big trouble — maybe he could find out important information.

Like if the Riders or Meanies were going to attack The Zone. Or if Yago was planning to ask Billy for another stupid thing to put on top of his Castle.

People liked information. People respected other people who had information they could use.

It was hard for Edward to blend into the Meanies' environment. There just wasn't a lot to blend into. Usually he didn't even think about how his powers worked but here he did. He'd decided that stretching out on the ground was good.

Edward watched the skin on his arms turn slightly shiny, smooth, and tannish. The texture was like superfine crystals.

About ten yards away there were about fifteen Blue Meanies, armor and all.

Edward didn't know what was going on, but he was pretty sure the Meanies were mad. Maybe scared, too, or something. Because their tentacles were flying around like crazy, like whips cracking in the air.

Edward remembered the terrible fight at the football stadium. His big brother had hidden him in the stands, but Edward had seen what was going on. He'd seen the Blue Meanies fire those weapons that shot lots of very sharp pieces of metal.

He'd seen one of the Meanies take aim at 2Face and he'd cried out, even though Jobs had told him to keep his mouth shut. 2Face had heard him and gotten out of the way just in time. 2Face had saved his life once, back when he'd been attacked by those ugly goblins and all, and Edward had figured he owed her.

Suddenly, the strange sound of the Meanies' waving tentacles got louder and Edward saw something new. A bunch of Meanies, no doubt armed with fléchette guns and mini-missiles, were approaching the first group. When they got closer, Edward saw that in the center of the second group was a Meanie without his armor. He looked like a prisoner. A wrinkly, funny-looking prisoner.

Edward watched. He'd learned a few of the signs the Meanies used to communicate, but when they were really upset like this it was hard to follow.

But he did figure out that the Meanie without the armor was in big trouble because one of the other Meanies tied his two tentacles together so he couldn't talk. Then everyone walked off, away from the edge of The Zone and toward the barracks.

Edward decided it would be too dangerous to follow the Meanies farther into their territory. Besides, he was scared. Maybe he could come back tomorrow and find out more, when the angry Meanies had calmed down.

Edward made his way back into The Zone. He was just stepping over the border when —

"Hey."

Edward jumped.

It was that guy who always followed Yago around. D-Caf. He was coming out of the woods. He was carrying a book.

Edward had heard Jobs say that D-Caf had killed someone. That made him a bad person.

D-Caf didn't look bad. Edward wondered if D-Caf was going to tell on him to Jobs. Jobs didn't like him sneaking off to spy.

"That was pretty cool," D-Caf said. "What you did. The way you can camouflage yourself and all."

"Yeah," Edward said warily.

"It makes you special."

Edward shrugged. "I guess."

D-Caf hung his head. He stuck the toe of his sneaker in the grassy ground and made circles. "I'd like to be special."

"My mom says —" Edward suddenly felt queasy, like when he had the flu that time.

"What?" D-Caf said, looking at Edward. "Oh. I don't remember my mom. She died way before the *Mayflower*."

Hearing that made Edward feel a little bit better.

Not that he was happy D-Caf didn't have a mother. Just that it gave them something in common.

"My mom says that everyone is special."

D-Caf smiled a bit at Edward. "She sounds nice, your mom."

Edward smiled. "She is."

(CHAPTER TEN)

SOMETHING DIDN'T MAKE SENSE.

If Mo'Steel hadn't known Jobs back on Earth, he might have been intimidated by his best friend's lab. By his best friend's *brain*.

As it was, Mo'Steel knew only the kind of respect and affection two guys felt for each other when they'd grown up in the same neighborhood, gone to the same school, thrown french fries at the jocks (behind their backs), and kidded each other about girls.

Jobs was the techie nerd. Mo'Steel was the risk-taking daredevil. Perfect match.

Mo'Steel picked up a thing made of metal and rubber and turned it over. And over. It looked a bit like the kind of fancy thermos you took camping. Sort of.

"What is this?" he asked finally.

Jobs looked up from the computer screen and

laughed. "Can't you tell? It's a model of a self-contained living unit. You know, there'd be no reason ever to leave. Even the food is provided by the unit."

Mo'Steel raised his eyebrows. His best friend was spending way too much time alone, floating around in deep space and holed up in his lab.

"Whatever you say, Duck," he said, putting down the thing. "You're the mad scientist, not me."

Jobs shrugged and went back to doing whatever it was he was doing.

Something had been on Mo'Steel's mind ever since Jobs had shown him the lumpy thing that might be Earth. He just couldn't wrap his head around Jobs's need to get back to the planet. Something didn't make sense.

Mo'Steel hopped up onto a worktable and put his hands on his knees.

"Got to ask you something, 'migo," he said.

Jobs grunted.

"Why is it so important to you, Jobs? To see if the planet is Earth. To try to make it work all over again. What do you hope to get out of it?"

The tapping of the keyboard fell silent. Mo'Steel waited. Then Jobs turned around.

"It's not all about going back to *Earth*," Jobs protested. "It's that . . . this place, it's *not* Earth. It's like a toy or a model or something. Let's face it, the level of programming it would take to create a fully functioning, totally lifelike world here is beyond Billy's capabilities. No insult to Billy. But even he knows he can't do it all."

Mo'Steel said, "Okay."

But Jobs wasn't finished.

"I just think we owe it to ourselves, to what's left of the human race, to start something new."

Jobs's tone was defensive. Mo'Steel didn't know how to take that.

"So, it's all about learning and discovery and challenge?" Mo'Steel asked.

His friend was silent.

"Duck?"

Jobs looked up at Mo'Steel. His eyes were tortured. "I can't explain it," he said raggedly. "Let it alone, Mo'. I just have to get back there. If I can."

They were gathered around the ship's elevator. Everyone but Billy, who was up in the attic, as usual.

The elevator was a structure that resembled a pyramid. It was a stack of square metal platforms, the bottom platform the largest, the top platform about the size of Jobs's bedroom back on Earth. On the top platform were three rows of three chairs each. Each chair sat on a raised, shallow disk. The mini-chair platforms were surrounded by semicircles of railing with narrow openings through which you could walk.

The whole structure looked old and worn.

It was Jobs who'd first guessed it was a form of transportation throughout the ship. It was Billy who, with the defeat of the Baby/Shipwright/Maker, had wrested full charge of the "elevator."

Jobs surveyed the lineup of volunteers. He was along for the ride. He was the one who'd promised Billy he'd go deep into Mother and find out what she — the ship — was keeping from him. Plus, his technical skills might come in handy.

Mo'Steel had jumped at the chance for an adventure. And face it, Jobs's best friend was daring and, okay, just a tiny bit reckless, too. But at the bottom of it all was an unbelievably large store of courage and Mo'Steel wasn't stingy about sharing it.

Of course Tamara was there as well. She was no longer a superhuman fighting machine, but she was still the only one with formal military training. She was a soldier. She could follow orders — and she could give them. So Tamara had volunteered.

Kubrick had also volunteered, but without the solemnity with which Tamara had. There was a sense of "nothing left to lose" with Kubrick. Jobs got the feeling he didn't really care one way or another what happened to himself or to the others. Kubrick had told Jobs, defiantly, that going on a mission was something to do, it would pass the time.

Anamull hadn't volunteered but Jobs had asked him to join the crew. He'd looked to Yago as if for permission, gotten it, and grinned. The kid was a bruiser and physical strength would be a definite asset down in the basement.

At first, Jobs was surprised when 2Face didn't ask to go along. Usually she wanted to be at the center of things, mostly because, as far as Jobs could tell, she was looking out for her own interests, watching her own back. Or actively politicking against, say, Yago, and for herself.

2Face wasn't all bad and she had suffered her share of discrimination since the *Mayflower* had been captured/saved by Mother, but Jobs thought she was a little too paranoid and cold-blooded for her own good. It didn't take him long to realize that 2Face had to have a motive for staying behind. What that motive was, exactly, he couldn't quite guess.

The final two members of the team were unlikely choices, but both Tate and Yago had wanted to come along. Jobs figured Tate was going because

Tamara was. It didn't matter to Jobs. He liked Tate, what little he knew of her. And for Tamara, Jobs felt a mix of pity and respect. It wasn't a totally comfortable feeling but it would have to do.

Yago's offering to be part of the mission was a mystery through and through. Generally, Yago was lazy and cowardly and completely self-interested. But since his up-close-and-personal experience with Mother, something about Yago had changed. Jobs couldn't tell if it was for the better, or even if Yago was faking his new demeanor. Still, nothing obvious explained Yago's volunteering, at least as far as Jobs could see.

Mo'Steel slapped him on the back.

"We're good to go."

Jobs nodded.

2Face would look out for Edward while Jobs was gone. Violet said she'd take in Roger Dodger for the time being. D-Caf said he'd be fine on his own.

There was nothing else holding them back.

"Let's go," Jobs said.

(CHAPTER ELEVEN)

"WHY ARE YOU HERE, YAGO?"

2Face watched Yago step onto one of the elevator's chair platforms with the rest of them. She stuck her hands in the pockets of her gray hooded sweatshirt and frowned.

She didn't know what Yago was up to with his newfound craziness. But it was probably something bad, especially for her. She couldn't figure out why he had chosen to go along with Jobs on his mission for Billy, either, but she was glad he'd gone. Because in his absence she was going to make some serious progress toward becoming the acknowledged and undisputed leader of this place. Not only of The Zone, but of the entire ship.

Billy had forced them all — the humans, the Riders, and the Meanies — to stop fighting and start talking. He had threatened them all with destruction between two gigantic walls and so everyone had shut up and listened. From that moment was born the Big Compromise, the uneasy truce under which all three groups now lived.

2Face hadn't wanted the truce. She still didn't. What 2Face wanted was to fight on, take over the entire ship, not share it with two alien species who could, at any moment, easily slaughter them.

What 2Face wanted was to dethrone Billy. He'd usurped the seat of power with his threat of annihilation. He'd forced this peace down their throats.

Billy was useful, sure. But 2Face wanted him to be useful under her control and command. Not under his own.

Now, with Jobs and Yago on their way to being temporarily out of sight, was her chance. 2Face didn't know how she was going to do it, but she knew she was going to come up with something.

She had to.

2Face watched as the team of seven descended into the stepped, pyramidlike body of the elevator, on their way down.

Maybe it wouldn't be too hard. The Remnants' current task, with Jobs, Yago, Kubrick, Mo'Steel, Anamull, Tate, and Tamara gone, was to make preparations for defense in the event of renewed hostilities on the part of the Riders or Blue Meanies.

And who's better at strategizing, 2Face thought, looking around at those who'd stayed behind, *than me?*

The group took the elevator to the lowest level of the ship. The ride took all of three minutes, longer than it would have if Billy hadn't slowed things down at Jobs's request. When they'd first found it, the elevator had operated at something close to the speed of light. It had caused a lot of motion sickness, to say the least.

No one spoke for the duration. But there was something Jobs wanted to know.

When the elevator stopped, they stepped off and into what they all called Mother's basement. It was a place that was very much like the dark, industrial-feeling basements they had known back on Earth.

Jobs turned to Yago.

"Why are you here, Yago?" he asked.

Yago smiled. The smile was calculated and hard. "It's pretty simple, Jobs," he answered. "I cannot pass up an opportunity to carry the truth to those who live in darkness."

Jobs thought, *Ooookay. That certainly clears things up,* and turned away shaking his head.

Anamull rubbed his nose and snorted loudly. "So, who's the big cheese here? Who's giving the orders?"

Pretty fair question, Jobs thought.

No one said anything. Jobs looked to each person in the group. And he noticed everyone else doing the same thing.

Kubrick? Probably not. He still creeped people out. Sad — but true.

Anamull? Nope. First, he wasn't very bright. Second, he was too prone to physical violence. Third, he was Yago's yes-man. Not leader material at all.

Yago. Well, guys like Yago had ruled nations back on Earth. But here, on board this ship, in Mother's basement, Yago was not going to get elected to any position of authority unless they all simultaneously lost their minds.

Tamara was tainted by her relationship with the Baby. And it didn't matter that none of it was her fault. The memories of her and the Baby were just too fresh. Too strong. Besides, as far as Jobs could tell, Tamara wasn't interested in being anyone's leader. She tended now to hang back until needed for a specific task, at which point she was willing enough to lend her support. But the hollow look in her eyes and her general silence told Jobs that she wasn't altogether there.

By association, Tate was not a possibility, either. Too close to Tamara.

Mo'Steel was by far the most physically courageous of the lot and his moral center was strong. Problem with choosing him was his long-standing friendship with Jobs. The perfect leader wouldn't be too closely tied to any of his followers. So there wouldn't be any favorites or the chance for sentimental thinking. But then again, wouldn't it be the same with Mo'Steel if Jobs were given control?

"What about you, Duck?" Mo'Steel said suddenly, breaking the silence. "You're the brainiac here."

Jobs was touched by Mo'Steel's vote. He knew he wasn't really leader material. But he'd do what he had to do.

"Let's just get this done," he said. "Let's just go with teamwork."

Again, no one said a word. And Jobs was grateful.

But he knew something was going on with Yago. Jobs didn't know exactly what, but he was definitely going to keep his eyes open.

CHAPTER TWELVE

"WE SHOULD STAY TOGETHER."

Yago didn't really notice his surroundings. He walked on with the others in the gloom occasionally brightened by the flickers from what Mo'Steel called the "projection booths," now under Billy's control.

Yago was very content. He'd learned patience and with patience had come rewards. Small at first, only a few followers, a few Chosen among Mother's former Children.

Yago had known for some time now that he was the One. Mother had not been able to defeat him, though she'd tried her best.

He was unconquerable because he was beautiful. He was whole. He was pure. He was the direct polar opposite of the Freaks, like 2Face and Kubrick, and he was the nemesis of their protectors, Mo'Steel and Jobs.

Yes, Yago had accepted the burden, responsibility, and glory of being the best of the survivors of the human race. And he'd chosen to include himself in this mission into Mother's hidden depths because the voice had told him to do so.

The voice.

It had also told him to bring along the gift given to him by Three Glowing Moons, one of his original followers. The voice had told him that he would find the perfect opportunity to use the special weapon.

Yago had learned patience. He knew he would recognize the opportunity when it presented itself.

"How long have we been walking?" Anamull sounded cranky. "I mean, how far away is this place, anyway?"

Jobs frowned. "Based on what Billy told me, I've estimated the ship is about 150 miles long by 100 miles wide. We're headed to the back of the ship and we started out pretty much midship, so . . ."

"That's a lot of miles." Mo'Steel shook his head. "I don't mind the exercise, but just walking along like this? Maybe I'll run or something. Meet you guys there."

"No." It was the first word Tamara had spoken since they'd started out. "We should stay together."

"I could be, like, the scout," Mo'Steel protested.

"I think we should listen to Tamara," Tate said.

"Me, too. We don't know what we're going to find down here," Jobs pointed out. "Especially since so much about Mother has changed since Billy took over."

Mo'Steel sighed. "Okay, I'm overruled. But I'm also bored. Maybe we could step up the pace?"

"Maybe we could rest?" Anamull suggested.

"Loser," Kubrick said.

"Freak."

"How about everybody just shutting up?!" Jobs snapped.

Anamull smirked. "Make me."

Jobs sighed. It was going to be a long walk.

CHAPTER THIRTEEN

"YOU'RE BREAKING THE RULES, BUDDY."

The basement held lots of memories for Kubrick. Bad ones. Even though he still didn't know if his — surgery — had taken place in the basement or somewhere else on the ship, it was where he and his father had found themselves abandoned. In the basement. It was where Kubrick had first encountered the unspeakable horror of himself. Where he had first had to deal with others and their disgusted/terrified expressions.

The basement was also the place where his father had gone crazy. No point in denying the troubled relationship they'd shared since Kubrick's first lousy day in school. No point in denying that Kubrick had partly resented having to take care of his suddenly helpless father. But there was also no point in denying that when Alberto had been killed, Kubrick had felt deep pain. And emptiness.

And now he was here again. When he asked himself, *Why?* he found himself answering, *Why not?*

They walked on, Kubrick in the lead. Then —

"Look!"

Kubrick stopped suddenly. The others fell into place behind him. Kubrick began to slowly advance toward the darkish marks on the floor ahead of him.

"I think it's blood," he said, his voice tight.

Kubrick knelt and peered closely at the print.

"It looks human. That's a swoosh — you know, a Nike mark in the middle of it." Kubrick stood and turned back to the others.

"Whoa. I mean, we've been hoping to run into more people, but not if they're, like, dead." Anamull. And he had made a good point.

They kept walking.

The view from the veranda was lovely, Violet couldn't deny that. Even if it wasn't real.

T.R. had told her something the other day. He'd shown up unexpectedly just as she was about to have lunch so she'd invited him in. They'd gotten to talking about things and at one point T.R. had explained the origin of the word *utopia*. It was from two Greek words meaning "no" and "place."

No place. Nowhere.

Just like where they all were, the Remnants of the human race. No place.

Violet's musings were interrupted just then by the sudden appearance in the distance of . . . Yes, of three Blue Meanies. She watched them get closer and it didn't take long to realize that they were on a direct course for her house.

But in a minute or two they'd be landing on the veranda.

Violet hurried inside and grabbed her link. She didn't even think about who to call.

"2Face? It's Violet. There's trouble. I think. Three Meanies are coming in over my house."

"I'll be right there," 2Face said.

Violet took a deep breath and went back outside to the veranda. This visit — if it was something so innocent — was unprecedented. Violet wasn't even sure it was allowed under the terms of the Big Compromise. If the Meanies had anything to say to the Remnants, shouldn't they go to Billy first?

Violet watched as the first Meanie landed a few yards away from her on the veranda. The other two remained in the air, circling slowly.

Without thinking, Violet waved hello. The Meanie did not respond with his tentacles but stood up on his hind legs to reveal the screen on the chest portion of his suit.

Violet read the words scrolled across the screen.

I am called Three Glowing Moons. I demand to see Yago.

"What?" Violet asked as she turned to see that 2Face and Edward — the latter nearly invisible against a line of potted trees — had arrived. Edward held something behind his back and stayed at the edge of the veranda.

"What does he want to see Yago for?" 2Face demanded.

"Why do you want to see Yago?" Violet asked the Meanie. She was getting a bad feeling in the pit of her stomach. She watched closely as the Meanie gesticulated with the two tentacles that extended from the side of his head. When he was finished she thought for a moment she'd misunderstood. She asked the Meanie to repeat himself. He did, with the help of a few words blipped across his screen.

"Okay." Violet took a deep breath. "It doesn't make a lot of sense, but this is what I got. They need to see Yago because they need 'the touch.' No, more like the laying on of hands. I think they're talking about some sort of ritual. And . . ."

"Come *on*, Violet," 2Face urged.

"Well, I think what they're saying is that 'the touch,' the ritual, brings joy."

"That's silly," Edward said with a giggle.

Violet hushed him. "No," she said. "I can understand. I think. It's not silly to them, Edward."

"I don't believe him," 2Face muttered. "What does Yago think he's doing?"

The Meanie repeated a series of gestures.

"He wants to see Yago," Violet said. "He says . . . he says he's made the required sacrifice so he must be allowed to see Yago."

"What does he mean by sacrifice?" 2Face asked.

Violet asked the Meanie for an explanation. When she got it, she wished she hadn't. Keeping an eye on the Meanies, she turned partway to 2Face. "This is bad," she said. "They've given Yago a fléchette gun."

"And he's . . . That's why he wanted to go on the mission. . . ."

Violet didn't know what 2Face was getting at.

2Face stepped forward. "Violet, tell our big blue friend the following: No, you cannot see Yago. You're breaking the rules, buddy. The Big Compromise? You're not supposed to be here. This is our place. You go back to your people right now, leave peacefully, and we'll forget this little visit ever happened. Okay?"

Violet communicated 2Face's message. The Meanie didn't seem very happy. Violet wished she were far, far away. Any place other than on the veranda acting as interpreter for three very determined aliens. "They say they don't care about the Big Compromise," she said, trying to keep her voice low and steady. "They say they need Yago. They say they won't take no for an answer."

CHAPTER FOURTEEN

"I WILL SEE YAGO."

Nope. He wasn't imagining it. What he'd been seeing wasn't random, wasn't a bunch of unrelated or disconnected structures. Jobs squinted and tried to see as far away as possible. Yes.

Something like a dotted line, running along the ceiling. Each dot was a pale blue circle, with . . . okay, something like a small knob in the center. Each dot was about ten feet from the next. Jobs turned slowly in a circle, following the dots with his eyes and thinking about what he'd seen previously. The line curved and branched. It was like looking at a subway map, sort of. Jobs walked on. He could see that the line continued unbroken beneath a transparent section of the ceiling, through which he could see the Riders' swamplike environment.

A rail line. Monorail. A form of transportation. Had to be. But how to use it?

In spite of Tamara's insistence that the group stay together — and his own agreement to the plan — Jobs found himself having fallen behind. No one was shouting out for him to hurry up, so he wasn't missed. Yet. Which was good because Jobs wanted to check out the strange objects he saw neatly stacked in a box.

There were about twenty of them. Carefully, Jobs picked the top one off the pile. It was almost weightless. It was also flexible, probably made of some terribly strong but superthin metal. Or plastic, Jobs couldn't tell which.

He didn't know if he was holding it right, but if he was, the object looked like an upside-down question mark. At the thin blunt end of the object was a small knob surrounded by a blue circle.

Jobs looked up at the line of circles and knobs that ran along the ceiling, then back down at the thing he held. It was worth a shot. He stuck the curve of the question mark under his right arm and with both hands gripped the long stem. Then he stepped directly under the line, pointed the knobbed end of the object up, and . . .

"Whoa!"

In a flash Jobs was pulled up into the air. The question mark had connected somehow with the line of dots and before he could catch his breath Jobs was zooming ahead.

When he was almost over his surprise, Jobs estimated he was moving at about twenty miles per hour along a type of monorail track. It was a high-speed shuttle, clearly constructed of an invisible power line to which the question mark had connected. Great. He'd catch up to the others in no time.

And then what? How do I stop this thing? How do I get off?

The group appeared not twenty yards ahead.

"Mo'!" Jobs shouted. In the distance, Mo'Steel stopped, turned, whooped with delight.

When Jobs was about ten yards away, it came to him.

"Look out!" he cried. "I'm coming down!"

One strong bounce and . . .

"WHAM!"

Jobs was on the floor.

Mo'Steel grinned. "Nice of you to drop in, Duck."

Back in the Zone, 2Face lunged but it was too late. In the blink of an eye the Meanie had wrapped a tentacle around Violet's neck.

"Violet, don't move!" she cried.

Violet's eyes were terrified. "I . . . ahhhhhh!"

2Face flinched. The Meanie had shocked Violet, jolted her with some sort of current that caused her face to go purple, her eyes to roll back in her head.

"Leave her alone!" 2Face screamed.

Violet slumped but the Meanie still held her tightly in his tentacle. With the other he signed a demand 2Face now easily recognized.

"I will see Yago."

"Don't . . ." Violet gasped, coming to.

Edward, where was Edward? 2Face saw him, just barely, against the whitewashed wall of Violet's house.

2Face thought fast. If she could rush past and around the Meanie, get behind him, startle him, maybe . . .

Too late.

A second Meanie landed directly in front of 2Face and drew his fléchette gun. Beyond him, the first Meanie held tightly to Violet.

2Face couldn't stand it, not being able to do something, anything.

"He . . ."

"Violet! No!"

"He's . . . basement."

2Face didn't have time to be mad at Violet or re-lieved that her suffering might soon be over. Because at that moment T.R. came running out through the back door of Violet's villa.

Her first thought was, *What is he doing here?*

Her second thought was to yell, "T.R.! Get out of here! Go get help!" And that's what she did.

But T.R. just stood there, mouth hanging open, frozen.

"T.R.!" 2Face screamed from behind the Meanie who had her at gunpoint. The Meanie didn't seem to care if she yelled, as long as she didn't try to get past him.

Still T.R. stood and gaped, eyes darting from Vio-let to 2Face.

Then —

"Aaahhhhh!"

Edward!

T.R.'s unexpected entrance had been enough of a diversion to allow Edward to move in on the Meanie who still held Violet. Even now, 2Face could see him only partially as he thrust his spear at the Meanie.

"Let her go!" he cried.

The Meanie seemed startled, if that was possible, and sidestepped Edward's thrust so that his armor was merely nicked.

"Edward, back off!" 2Face yelled. A six-year-old kid with a handmade spear was obviously no match for an armed alien.

Still gripping Violet in one tentacle, the Meanie drew his fléchette gun and fired wildly, madly.

Violet screamed.

2Face squeezed her eyes shut and said, "Oh, please, please, let him be okay."

Then she opened them.

The shots had somehow missed Edward. He was safe, climbing to his feet. But they had found a target in T.R.

"Take that, you big jerk!" Edward cried. And to 2Face's amazement, Edward charged the Meanie again. The kid was panting, tears streaming down his face, snot running from his nose, he was obviously scared and tired, but 2Face watched as the Meanie crashed to the floor, releasing Violet as it did.

The Meanie guarding 2Face lowered his weapon in surprise. He looked up to his hovering companion, back to his fallen colleague, then up again to the other Meanie.

"I think it's time you got out of here," 2Face said quietly. Even if it didn't understand her exact words, she *knew* the meaning was clear.

The Meanie lifted off. The remaining Meanie followed. And they flew away.

The entire encounter had taken less than fifteen minutes.

CHAPTER FIFTEEN

"PERSONALLY, I'M ENJOYING THIS."

They'd found more of the question marks. Now the seven of them were moving along, all in a row, toward the dark place Billy had asked Jobs to check out.

Mo'Steel was having a blast. He was on the lead question mark. He only half listened to the conversation behind him.

"You know what I feel like?" Anamull said, "You know what we look like? Like shirts on an old-fashioned dry cleaner's rack. You know the kind — the guy presses a button and the shirts go revolving and when your number comes up, the guy stops the machine and takes the shirt off."

"Or pants," Tate said. "Could be pants."

"Or a dress uniform." Tamara.

"This has got to be the most boring conversation I have ever heard," Jobs said. He was near the rear of their line, just ahead of Tamara. "Ever."

Kubrick smirked. "You got a better topic? Huh? Maybe something that will take our minds off the fact that we don't know where we're going or what's waiting for us when we get there."

"Or to purity," Yago said cryptically.

Mo'Steel sighed. He wished Yago would shut up about the purity thing. It was already past getting old.

"Personally, I'm enjoying this," Mo'Steel announced to no one. "Could be faster, could have some loops and whatnot, but hey, it still works for me. Definitely something the *Mo'Run* doesn't have."

"Mo'Steel, you get bored pretty easily, don't you?" Tate asked.

Mo'Steel remembered the awesome, impossible-in-the-real-world fighting moves Billy's mind control had allowed him to execute back when control of the ship's bridge was totally up in the air.

Back before the Big Compromise.

He hadn't been bored then.

The Meanies were gone but Violet was angrier than 2Face had ever thought her capable of being.

2Face had never seen Violet so furious, so absolutely enraged. And 2Face was impressed. Anger was power. Anger was energy. Anger let you do things you wouldn't ordinarily do.

As for herself, she was angry, too, and also scared, which was smart. Fear was good because it kept you on guard.

The moment had finally come, just as she had known it would. Her chance was finally here. Her chance to prove once and for all that she, 2Face, should be in charge of their little band of Remnants.

She'd been handed a vital piece of information by the Blue Meanies: Yago had obviously made contact with the enemy. Yago had accepted a weapon.

She had to move fast. "Strike while the iron is hot," she muttered. Only question now was how to use both the dirt on Yago and the reality of the Meanies' atrocity to her advantage.

Zipping along on this one-way track to the dark place allowed Tamara way too much time to think. She far preferred action to thought, but not the kind of wild action Mo'Steel liked. Tamara liked focused, directed action, action with a specific goal.

She hoped she'd find such action soon.

Tamara hoped she'd have a chance to show Jobs and the others that she was worth something. She hoped for an opportunity to prove that without the Baby she could still be powerful — and better, powerful on her own terms. An independent person.

Sometimes she missed the Baby. Not really the Baby as it had actually been but her baby as she imagined it might have been. If Earth hadn't been destroyed by an asteroid. If five hundred years aboard the *Mayflower* hadn't caused such a gross mutation.

If that's what the Baby had been, a mutation of a normal human being. And not something else entirely. A Shipwright. A Maker. An alien.

Tamara knew she'd never even be just one of the group, just another of the Remnants. She wasn't paranoid. She was pretty sure that most of the others didn't actively or consciously hate her. But she was also pretty sure they didn't accept her as one of their own.

Burroway and T.R. were the coldest. Burroway simply ignored her. T.R. wanted to psychoanalyze her, see how her bizarre experience had affected her ego or whatever. He saw her as an experiment, as the unique subject of a prizewinning article he would never see published.

The women, Dr. Cohen and Olga Gonzalez, they

were nice. Nicer than Tamara thought she might be in their shoes. For that, she was grateful. Still, neither had asked her over for coffee. Neither had asked her about her old life back on Earth.

Jobs and Mo'Steel were good kids. Violet and Noyze, too. Tamara didn't trust 2Face but she got the feeling that's the way 2Face wanted it. Anamull, D-Caf, Roger Dodger — Tamara hardly noticed them. Certainly not as any major threat to her living peacefully in The Zone.

So maybe no one really loathed and despised her, that was good. But no one was warm and fuzzy, either.

Except for Tate.

Tate went out of her way to make Tamara feel welcome, accepted, loved even. She was a good kid, sixteen or seventeen, Tamara guessed. Sometimes Tamara felt bad about letting Tate care for her so lovingly, so unselfishly. Almost as if she were Tate's older sister or aunt.

And that was flattering, but Tamara didn't feel the same way about Tate. Sometimes she thought she should confront Tate with the truth, kind of say how much she appreciated her friendship, but the Baby had changed Tamara. Changed her way of feeling toward others.

Tamara craned her neck to see Tate up ahead on the track, just behind Mo'Steel. But it was nice to have someone care.

Still, they zipped along.

Tamara didn't think she needed to prove anything to Tate. But she did want to prove to the others that she was so very sorry for all the trouble she had caused. She wanted to atone for her actions while under the Baby's control.

That's why she'd volunteered for this mission. And she seriously hoped she'd have a chance to make things right.

If the stupid track ever ended.

(CHAPTER SIXTEEN)

"WHY ALL THE SECRECY?"

Violet went first. 2Face had expected her to balk at the dramatic entrance she'd planned, but Violet was still too furious to say no to such a bold and confrontational move.

Everybody was there. Everybody but Billy, who didn't attend general meetings. Billy rarely — if ever — left the attic. That was fine by 2Face. Right now, she wanted — needed — to be center stage.

"Why all the secrecy?" Burroway demanded.

"Why aren't we meeting at the town center, like usual?" Noyze asked worriedly.

2Face heard them all, the nervous rustling, the whispered questions. Anticipation was high. She'd set the scene.

Things could be worse. Tate looked back over her shoulder and caught a glimpse of Tamara's booted left foot, her leg in olive-green pants. Still there, bringing up the rear, the only one on the mission who was armed.

Though Tate respected Sergeant Tamara Hoyle's chosen profession, she fervently hoped there'd be no need for guns.

Behind Tate, Anamull began to sing.

"Shut up!" Kubrick said.

"Dude, didn't you ever go to camp? Just passing the time."

"I never went to camp. My father didn't believe in it."

"What? Did he think you were too good to hang with kids like me?" he challenged. "Yeah, I can see you giving someone a superatomic wedgie. Right."

Tate blocked out their stupid argument and concentrated on what was ahead. And on how to swallow her fear of the unknown.

Tate had never been one to give up easily. She wasn't about to start now.

Everyone had gathered around T.R.'s body. To pay their last respects, 2Face supposed, though it was general knowledge that nobody had much liked T.R. He'd been kind of a weenie, actually.

2Face watched from afar and let her mind wander.

She thought Burroway's house, like the man himself, was pretentious beyond all bounds of tolerance. The guy imagined himself as some wealthy, eccentric, probably titled English gentleman, with his pipes and bookshelves stocked with leather-bound volumes, and afternoon tea, and three cartoon servants who called him "sir."

2Face snatched another tea biscuit from the silver serving tray and settled into what was certainly Burroway's throne, a very comfy, high-backed leather chair, set right by the roaring fire.

Time to call this meeting to order.

CHAPTER SEVENTEEN

"WE'RE GOING HOME, PEOPLE.
WE'RE GOING HOME."

With unasked-for help from Violet and Edward, 2Face told the group what had happened on Violet's veranda.

"This is Yago's fault. No one listened to me before; everyone has to listen now."

Silence.

"This is only the beginning," 2Face went on. "The Children will be back. And they'll be back in force. This is not a game. We have to be ready for them. We have to be prepared to defend ourselves. We have to show the Children that we are not intimidated by their murderous, unprovoked attacks.

"Even if you didn't like T.R., he was one of us."

2Face paused, lowered her head for a moment as if contemplating what she'd just said, then looked up again, eyes purposefully fierce.

"The ship is ours," she declared. "Like Billy said, we are a mere six months away from what most likely is planet Earth. Our home. Now, I know that in the past I've agreed on making Mother, the ship, our true home. For making all of it our home and ours exclusively. Unlike Jobs, I didn't agree to locating Earth or some other habitable planet and establishing a colony on it. But the time for petty differences is over." 2Face continued. "True, we're only six months from home but a lot can happen in that time. So there can't be any more divisions. No more separate camps. We have to join together against our enemies and survive these next months. We have to take all of the ship for our own purposes. We have to get her back to Earth. There we can use Mother's power — the power of *our* ship — to help restore the glory of human civilization."

Burroway laughed but it wasn't a happy sound. "Pretty words, 2Face — 'restore the glory of human civilization.' How long have you been practicing that speech?"

2Face ignored him.

"Violet?" It was Olga. "You're okay with this? I thought you . . ."

"I'm with 2Face," Violet said firmly.

"I say we should wait for Jobs and the others to get back before we make any decisions that are going to affect us all," Dr. Cohen said.

Noyze nodded. "I agree."

"Me, too," said Olga.

"Well, there might be a problem with that," 2Face said. "Ordinarily, I'd agree with you," she lied. "But I learned today that Yago traded weapons with the Blue Meanies. He's armed with an enemy fléchette gun." 2Face paused to let the information sink in. "Think about it. Given Yago's state of mind, what are the odds that Jobs and the others are still alive?"

Violet's expression was icy.

Noyze blurted, "They can't be dead!"

Burroway put his head in his hands and said, voice breaking, "What is happening to us?"

Olga's face was pale. "Look, the three of us, myself, Dr. Cohen, and Burroway, think we shouldn't make any major moves just yet. We —"

"Nice try," 2Face interrupted, "but we're the majority here, Ms. Gonzalez."

More silence.

Burroway broke the silence.

"What are we going to do with . . . ?" He looked

meaningfully at T.R.'s shrouded body. "He can't stay here."

Dr. Cohen sighed. "Can we bury him? I can't believe I'm asking this, but the soil is fake and not very deep . . ."

"We can ask Billy to make a small mausoleum," Violet suggested.

"Yes, that's probably best."

2Face stood. "I'm going to see Billy," she announced.

"Why?" Burroway.

"Why do you think? To tell him our decision. And to ask him to turn this ship around, head it for Earth. We're going home, people. We're going home."

(CHAPTER EIGHTEEN)

"END OF THE LINE."

Jobs should have known. Even here in space, Murphy's Law still worked. If something can go wrong, it will.

They'd been riding along peacefully for some time when . . .

"What the . . . ?"

Ahead of them by only about three or four yards the ceiling was beginning to burn. A small, ragged, charred hole, then bigger, then bigger.

"Something's trying to get through up there!" Kubrick shouted.

And they were headed right for that something.

"Get down!" Tamara shouted. "Get down! Now!"

They did. Tamara and Tate, Yago and Anamull, Jobs and Mo'Steel and Kubrick each released, and fell to the floor.

Just as hundreds of gallons of water came gushing through the hole in the ceiling, smashing down onto the floor.

"Well, this isn't boring!" Mo'Steel yelled over the roar of the water. "I think we're finally gonna see some action!"

Three Blue Meanies came through the hole. The second they had passed through the ceiling, the hole was being repaired from above. The water slowed down and then stopped.

"They knew exactly where to find us," Jobs whispered to the others.

The Blue Meanies came closer. The one in the center seemed to be the leader or spokesperson. The two Meanies flanking him held their front legs raised, weapons at the ready.

The leader rose on his hind legs and scrolled a sentence across the screen on his chest.

Jobs read it aloud: "I am Five Revolving Planets. We are here to take the one you call Yago."

"Take him?" Tamara demanded. "For what?"

"They can't do that, can they?" Tate whispered worriedly. "What about the Compromise?"

"Why?" Jobs asked. He told himself to stay calm.

Five Revolving Planets displayed another sentence.

The charge is blasphemy.

"What?!" Mo'Steel.

Jobs shot a look at Yago, whose face was a serene blank. "Look," Jobs said to the Meanie, "I think you'd better explain."

The Meanie did, with slowly scrolling words as well as the sign language most of the Remnants had come to understand to a certain extent.

He has violated the Big Compromise, which specifically states that the humans will do nothing to interfere with the practice of the Children's rites and rituals. This one you call Yago has presented himself as the god of the Children, thereby urging the Children to deny their ancient faith in Mother.

"Yago?" Jobs said, stomach sinking. "What have you been telling the Meanies?"

Yago smiled enigmatically. "I have only spoken the truth," he said.

Yeah, Jobs said angrily to himself. *The truth according to a nut case.* He said, "Anamull, did you know about this?"

Anamull looked distinctly sheepish. "Well, yeah, kind of," he admitted. "But, I mean, me and D-Caf, we thought it was all a big goof. We thought it was pretty funny. You know, Yago's whacked, man. You should hear the crazy things he says."

Jobs fought the urge to smack Anamull in the back of the head.

"Look, this is pretty serious," he said to the head Meanie. "I'm not denying it, but I am saying we should all hold a meeting, something formal, back in The Zone."

"Yeah, you can't just take one of us prisoner whenever you want to," Kubrick said. "What about a trial?"

Are you refusing to hand over this criminal? Five Revolving Planets demanded.

Jobs looked at Yago. His face wore that annoying, blissed-out look. *Maybe they should just let the Meanies take him*, Jobs thought. He'd been fed up with Yago since the very beginning.

But no. Yago was one of them. Okay, an obnoxious one, but they had a duty to protect him as they would protect a well-liked member of their group.

Even when the odds for success — in this case, three armored aliens with powerful weapons against seven humans, only one of whom was armed — were not good, to say the least.

Jobs looked at Tamara. She hesitated, then nodded.

"That's right," Jobs said, turning back to the Meanie. "We won't turn him over to you here."

I am afraid you have no choice, Five Revolving Planets replied. *This blasphemer —*

"I will go with you."

Jobs whirled.

"You *what?!*" Kubrick asked in disbelief.

Yago stepped forward.

"I will go and face my accusers. I have nothing to hide. I have nothing for which to be ashamed." Yago paused. "I have but one request at this time."

Five Revolving Planets signaled impatiently for Yago to go on.

"I would like to leave something of myself behind for my companions. In the event that I do not return to their side, I would wish to be remembered as their friend."

Five Revolving Planets seemed to consider Yago's request. A moment later, he signed his permission.

Jobs didn't see what was coming, though later he knew he should have.

Yago took a small backpack off his shoulders. Slowly, he reached inside . . .

Oh no . . . Jobs said silently.

Yago whipped the fléchette gun from the backpack and before Jobs could get the word out —

"No!" — one Blue Meanie was downed, another wounded.

Five Revolving Planets was unharmed. With practice, it drew its own fléchette gun. Jobs knew it was also probably equipped with a mini-missile or two.

This was not, however, the time or place to find out.

Suddenly, the injured Meanie collapsed against Five Revolving Planets.

"Come on!"

It was Tamara, grabbing Jobs, herding him before her, shouting now, "Run," her own handgun drawn, Yago's fléchette gun tucked in her belt.

They ran. Continuing in the direction they'd been headed when the Meanies had broken through the ceiling.

Jobs's feet pounded the cold basement floor. *Great*, he thought. *So much for being careful.* He'd hoped to approach the dark place with caution, not with cries and shouts and gunshots.

The awful killing whir of a fléchette gun!

Kubrick was hit! Jobs expected a shout of pain but none came. Kubrick just kept charging on and with a lurch of his stomach, Jobs realized that Kubrick was unaware of the wound.

"Kubrick!"

He looked over at Jobs. Jobs pointed to the wound. "Here!" he shouted, tearing off his jacket and tossing it to Kubrick. "Wrap it tight."

Kubrick looked up from his bleeding left wrist to Jobs. His eyes were dull. But he caught the jacket with his right hand, didn't miss a step, kept running.

"Everyone!" Tamara pointed ahead to another stack of upside-down question marks. "Get back on the monorail thing!"

Fine by me, Jobs thought. He skidded to a stop, grabbed a question mark, tossed one to Tate, tumbling up beside him, and got on.

Jobs looked over his shoulder. Tate was just behind him, followed by Kubrick, holding on awkwardly with one hand, then Yago, Anamull, then Mo'Steel, with Tamara in the rear, taking careful shots at the two pursuing Meanies.

He faced forward. He couldn't see anything in the distance, no sign of their destination, just more gray space with patches of darker gray and small beams of light.

How long would this go on?

Briefly Jobs wondered if the four-legged Meanies could ride the monorail. He looked back again. They were still coming at them on foot. No monorail. And they weren't flying, so maybe the ceiling was too low or the atmosphere wrong for flight.

The Meanies were fast on all fours, but not as fast as they could be in the air. Good.

A horrible squeal like a bottle rocket!

Jobs flinched. Tate screamed and he caught a glimpse of her over his shoulder. Her question mark's connection to the rail had been severed and she'd fallen to the ground.

"Run!" he shouted unnecessarily.

More ear-shattering squeals!

Another mini-missile, the kind that had "gotten" Yago back at the football stadium.

"We are in deep doo-doo!" Mo'Steel shouted.

"I'm down!" Kubrick.

"Get Tate!" Jobs cried, automatically hunching as best he could to avoid being hit in the head by enemy fire.

"Look!"

Ahead, just about ten yards. Now nine. The dark place. Had to be. But . . .

There was no wall — at least nothing visible. Instead there was suddenly a space of bright white light and chill air Jobs could feel on his face from some distance away.

Closer. Closer. Now Jobs could see a figure . . . a

woman, standing completely still and untroubled in the midst of the light.

Closer . . .

"Ahh!"

With a knee-jarring thud, Jobs crashed at the very feet of the woman. Behind him he heard the grunts of the others piling up, heard two pairs of feet slapping along, then stopping.

"End of the line," Jobs muttered, climbing slowly to his feet.

CHAPTER NINETEEN

"THE SOLITARY LIFE IS NOT ALL IT'S CRACKED UP TO BE, IS IT?"

2Face had come to see him on the bridge. Billy had not been expecting her so soon. He'd seen the Blue Meanies' violation of their agreement. He'd known of T.R.'s death and the meeting the others had held.

But he'd been hoping that Jobs would return before 2Face came to see him with her demand.

Jobs and the others . . . Billy had lost them. He hoped that meant they had succeeded in penetrating the dark place. He hoped they would come back with the answers he sought.

He would just have to wait.

"Billy, something's happened."

2Face stood looking down on Billy in his reclining chair.

"I know," he said.

"Then you also must know that we've voted not

to wait. We've voted to turn the ship around right now. We want to head for Earth."

"I . . . I'm not sure it's a good idea," Billy said.

2Face exploded. "We were attacked, Billy! T.R. is dead. We've got a traitor in our midst and who knows the extent of the damage he's done."

"We can take precautions. . . ."

"No. It's time to go on the offensive. Take control of the ship completely. Forget the Big Compromise!"

Billy got up from his chair. He moved farther away from 2Face.

"It will mean trouble," he said. "I told Jobs I might not be much help in an all-out war. There are restrictions." Billy felt himself threatened. It was insane. He had so much power, he was in charge of so much, but this girl scared him.

"I want to talk to Jobs," he said. He couldn't even meet her eyes. Why was he so disturbed by her? "I want to wait until he gets back. I want to know what he has to say."

"You *want?!*" 2Face shouted. Billy flinched. "What does it matter, Billy, what *you* want? I speak for everyone, Billy. I speak for us all."

Billy didn't like the way 2Face put things. He didn't want to think about himself, his role, in a blatantly political context. He wasn't some elected official back on Earth, some paid representative, someone who thought of constituents and funding and campaigning.

He was . . . what he was. And Jobs was going to help him find out what exactly that was.

Billy turned away from 2Face.

"What's it going to be, Billy? Are you one of us? Or have you decided that you don't need us anymore? Is that it, Billy? Because you need to think long and hard about being on your own. The solitary life is not all it's cracked up to be, is it? Who knows that better than you, Billy, am I right? Five hundred years alone, all alone." 2Face sighed. "You were in really sorry shape, my friend, when we found you. Sad and sorry shape. Personally, I can't imagine anyone wanting to go through that horror again, but hey, that's me. Right, Billy?"

Billy shook his head but turned around. Those long and horrible waking years. No, he couldn't endure that again, no.

2Face walked slowly toward him. Her voice was low. "We carried you when you were a helpless, comatose lump, Billy. It would have been so easy for us to just abandon you."

For the first time in centuries, Billy felt tears prickling at his eyes.

"But we didn't abandon you, Billy. Even when we didn't know if you'd ever revive, we kept you alive and safe from harm."

Through a haze of confused emotion, Billy realized that 2Face was very close.

"How can you be so ungrateful?" she whispered. "How can you turn your back on us now?"

How could he . . . He shook his head. He wanted to say something. He didn't know what.

2Face came closer. She was looking at him. Billy closed his eyes and the tears spilled down his cheeks.

Her hands were gentle and they wiped the tears from his face. "I see," she whispered. "I see."

She took his hand and led him to his chair and sat by his side. She held his hand. Her voice was gentle. It lulled him.

"You're one of us, Billy. A human being. You're not some machine, in spite of what you might think all alone up here with no one to talk to about the really important stuff. But you're not alone, Billy. And you never have to be alone again."

CHAPTER TWENTY

"WHAT DOES SHE KNOW THAT WE DON'T?"

"Whoa." Mo'Steel came to stand by Jobs. "A beautiful mystery woman. She's, like, out of a fairy tale."

"No happy ending yet," Tamara said. "They're coming."

Jobs whirled around. The two remaining Meanies were closing in. The one in front, the injured one, raised his fléchette gun, took aim at Yago, kept coming closer, stopped within feet of his target, while Jobs and the others stood as if paralyzed, pulled the trigger . . .

Nothing. The gun was empty.

Yago motioned to Anamull, who came out of his paralysis, grabbed the Meanie's gun, tossed it to Tamara. Then he wrenched one of the Meanie's tentacles out of the blue-black suit.

The woman said nothing, displayed no reaction.

Yago stepped forward. Jobs was mesmerized.

Yago reached out and lightly touched the exposed tentacle and . . . Anamull released him.

The Meanie went into a swoon.

"What the . . . ?" Kubrick muttered.

Mo'Steel cleared his throat nervously.

"Good lord," Tate breathed.

The mystery woman remained impassive.

And then — the second Meanie, the leader. Five Revolving Planets.

Everything happened in fast-forward. Before Tamara could take aim, before anyone could duck or cry out, the Meanie leader shot its companion. With a clatter, the injured Meanie fell to the ground.

Five Revolving Planets turned its weapon on Yago. Its tentacles thrashed furiously. Yago stood completely still and unprotesting.

And then . . . from behind Jobs and the others came a loud and bubbling gush of . . .

As one, Jobs, Tate, Tamara — dragging Yago — Mo'Steel, Anamull, and Kubrick dashed out of its path.

It was everything from a bad dream, a scary movie.

It was disgusting and repulsive. Someone gagged. Then someone else. The smell was atrocious and offensive and almost worse of an assault than the sight. It was a seething mass of just plain gross.

It was the woman.

As Jobs and Mo'Steel and the others watched, horrified, fascinated, the seething, vile mass began to spread outward, in the direction of Five Revolving Planets, who had turned his fléchette gun on Yago. It oozed and ran and seeped until it covered the Meanie's four legs. Immediately, Five Revolving Planets began to disappear.

It took all of sixty seconds.

And then, in a flash, the woman was back, her body whole, her loveliness intact. Long dark hair, sparkling gray eyes, a nearly perfectly symmetrical face.

It didn't matter. Jobs had seen what he'd seen. His revulsion must have still shown on his face.

The woman grinned. "Don't be so squeamish! The human body is designed to excrete and secrete all manner of parasites, viruses, bacteria, fungi. You must know that from Biology, hmm? Well, the evolved human body can turn that mundane reality into a weapon. I simply cleansed all the filth from my body, cultured it at an accelerated rate, and caused it to migrate onto — or, if you prefer, to get rid of — the creature who was threatening you."

"Who are you?" Tate demanded.

"Or what?" Jobs added.

"Well, young man, you are direct! My name is

Amelia." The woman laughed and her laugh was like ice tinkling in a glass. "It's my real name, don't look so shocked."

"Where did you come from? I mean —"

"I'm from Chicago. Go, Cubs!"

No one laughed. No one smiled.

"Oh, of course. I see what you mean," Amelia taunted. "Well, like you, I came to this ship on the *Mayflower*."

Silence.

"Hmm. Don't you even want to know why I was chosen for the *Mayflower Project?*" Amelia asked. "What I did back on Earth that made me so special as to be considered one of the Chosen?"

"It doesn't really matter," Tamara said abruptly.

"No? Well, okay. All right, then. Let's not be friends. At least, not right away. There's time. And someday we will all be together, all of you and the three of us."

"Three?" Jobs said. "There were eight people missing from the *Mayflower*. What happened to the other five?"

"You assume I know — and I do. Sadly, they were unable to make the transition."

"What transition?" Kubrick demanded, clutching his wrist to his chest. "Are they dead?"

"My, but you are impatient."

"Look, tell us what you know or —"

"My companions are not far away." There was an unmistakable threat in Amelia's tone.

"I asked you before: What are you?" Jobs tried to keep his voice calm, his tone rational. "You and the other two."

"We are human. Well, formerly human." Amelia frowned and paused as if to consider her words. Jobs knew it was a game. "Let's just say my companions and I are human a few miles farther along the road than you. But don't despair, you're coming along. Most of you, anyway. Some of you are already on the evolutionary path and are moving at quite a good clip. And Billy —"

"You know about Billy." It was a statement more than a question. It was also a challenge.

Amelia closed her eyes. When she spoke, her voice had taken on a strange, wondering quality. "Oh, yes, I know all about Billy. As I was saying, Billy is already quite close to us. In fact, he will soon be just like us."

Jobs shook his head. "Evolutionary path. Evolution is a long, slow process. Major changes, changes like . . ." Jobs looked at his companions, nodded at Amelia. "They don't happen this fast. Not in a few months. Not even in five hundred years." Jobs suddenly felt frightened. He thought of Edward. Of the Baby. Yago, too? "Not without some help," he said.

Amelia opened her eyes. Jobs thought, *If looks could kill . . .*

"Some 'help'?" she spat. "What you so innocently call help is the greatest force in the galaxy. In this or any other galaxy!" Amelia took a deep breath and started again. This time, her tone was less intense. "But you'll understand soon enough. Most of you. And the rest . . ."

Amelia shrugged. "Now, leave us. Go back to Billy. Tell him what you found here. And tell him this: He must not alter the ship's course. The Earth you seek no longer exists. It is long dead and gone. So tell Billy he must not, under any circumstances, alter course."

Jobs made no promise.

Amelia glared at him. "I mean it," she said.

Jobs nodded imperceptibly. It was enough for the mystery woman from Chicago.

Jobs and the others watched as Amelia turned and calmly walked away from them. They watched until Amelia could no longer be seen in the flare of a too-bright light.

"Scary chick," Mo'Steel said finally.

"Seriously." Jobs hesitated. "But also scared."

Mo'Steel chuckled. "Uh, not of you, Duck."

"I know. She's scared of Billy. Maybe she's scared of the missing five, too. She didn't say they were dead. Three against five. And against all of us, allied with Billy. I don't know, Mo'. Amelia might be scary but she's a lousy liar."

Kubrick was angry. "What does she know that we don't? Why shouldn't Billy change course? Let's follow her. . . ."

"No." Jobs put his hand on Kubrick's good arm. On the long-sleeved denim shirt he always wore, buttoned to the neck. "Not now."

"Then when?" Kubrick demanded, pulling away.

Jobs thought. "Soon," he said quietly. "Maybe very soon."

CHAPTER TWENTY-ONE

IT WAS REAL BUT IT HAD TO BE FAKE.

They headed back toward the elevator that would take them up to The Zone. They decided to skip the monorail and walk. It was a solemn crew.

No one spoke to Yago. Tamara walked just behind him, hand on her gun. The others kept their distance. Jobs had no idea what they were going to do about Yago when they got back to Billy. No one had suggested so far that the few Remnants of the human race establish a new code of conduct for life aboard Mother. There were no written laws and there was no judicial or penal system. Which came down to meaning that none of them was protected, guilty or innocent.

Mob rule? Prairie justice?

Yago was keeping quiet on their homeward journey. He might be nuts, but he wasn't stupid. Jobs would give him that.

By some unspoken agreement, Jobs had emerged as a sort of leader. Especially since the encounter with Amelia, who'd addressed most of her comments to him. It was okay by Jobs, being the temporary leader. He was sick and he was tired and all he wanted was to get them all back home.

Funny, he thought, plodding along, *what you call home when you've been through a nightmare.*

And then . . .

There was a deep shudder that seemed to come from under their feet and over their heads, too. *There was something animal-like in the sound,* Jobs thought, though he knew that was wrong, something low and frightened. *Maybe it's me who's frightened.*

"What was that?" Tate said when it had stopped.

"I think I know." Jobs frowned. "But I wish I didn't."

He walked ahead a few steps, stopped, squinted, then put his hand in the air.

"Over here. Let's go!"

"What is it?" Tamara said, the first to follow, pulling Yago along with her.

It looked like nothing more than a dark and narrow hole in one of the ship's walls.

"2Face showed me after Billy took charge of Mother," Jobs said. "She and Edward accidentally fell through one of these tubes. They're part of the original architecture of the ship."

"What are they for?" Mo'Steel asked.

Jobs shrugged. "We're still not sure. Maybe for performing maintenance on the outside of the ship. Though that seems unlikely. Maybe just for fun. Some sort of extravehicular activity, anyway. Doesn't matter now. We can get outside the ship, see what's happening."

Another deep shudder, this one lasting longer than the first.

"I want to go," Kubrick said.

Jobs nodded. "Good."

Kubrick held up the stump, all that remained of his left hand. Miraculously, it had stopped bleeding. "This doesn't bother you?"

"Not if it doesn't bother you," Jobs replied impatiently. "Mo'Steel, you're coming, too. And Tamara. Okay?"

Mo'Steel grinned. "Ready for the ride, 'migo."

Yago, Tate, and Anamull stayed behind. Jobs took Anamull aside and told him to keep an eye on Yago. To subdue him if necessary, like if he tried to move on alone. Anamull seemed unnerved enough to obey Jobs's order.

Then Jobs took Tate aside and told her to keep

an eye on both Anamull and Yago. If they took off without her, she was to come after Jobs in space. After some hesitation, Tamara gave her pistol to Tate with brief instructions and a stern warning about the safety.

Tate's eyes shone. "You can trust me," she said. "The both of you."

Jobs nodded. "I know."

He turned to the others.

"It's going to be — weird," Jobs said to the small crew. "2Face said there was a drop."

"A drop?"

"A big one," Jobs affirmed. "Mo'Steel, you first. Then Kubrick, me, Tamara last. One by one, but don't be too slow."

"Wait. Are we sure this thing still works?" Kubrick said. Jobs noted fear in his green eyes. "We're not pitching ourselves out into space just to die, are we?"

"Only one way to find out." Mo'Steel stepped into the black hole that was the tube's mouth.

Kubrick hesitated a split second, then followed.

Jobs fought down a surge of panic and took a giant step into the dark beyond.

If Tamara followed, Jobs wasn't aware of it. Nor was he aware of Mo'Steel or Kubrick. All he was aware of was himself falling, falling, tumbling head over heels, and still falling.

Jobs tried to scream but nothing came out. Or else the sound of his own blood rushing in his ears blocked out the sound of his voice.

And still he fell, past flashes of dark red shapes and spooky forms and . . .

Jobs felt like he was choking, like he was suffocating. Dimly he recalled 2Face's telling him about this part, about having to pass through something that felt like warm taffy, being coated with it, head to toe.

Then — he was out! He could breathe again, he could see, but he couldn't hear much. It was like his ears were stuffed with cotton. And all over him, coating every inch, was a sticky, pliable covering.

The goo space suit. It would allow Jobs — and the others, close by — to move through space. If it worked the way it should, it would keep them safe from any massive storm of radiation or the incredible heat of a hurtling fireball, if there were even meteors in this star system, or the deadly cold of space, or the blinding brightness of a sun.

This was not the first time Jobs had been here, but the experience still overwhelmed him. Jobs felt panic begin to seep through his brain. He couldn't find the hole through which they'd exited the ship.

Maybe it was no longer there, had closed up. If so, Jobs fervently hoped it would open again when they wanted to get back inside.

Jobs flipped or found himself flipping — he couldn't tell which.

The ship itself, seen from this interesting perspective, was vast, an eternal topography of metal forms and sparking lights, of bulges and bubbles and neon in yellow and red. It was almost cartoonlike. It reminded Jobs of a hand-constructed model that could easily fit into a shoe box — and at the same time appear massive on a wide screen.

It was real but it had to be fake. Just like everything on board or about Mother, Jobs thought. Another angle from which to see the world. Get used to it.

Ahead — what Jobs thought was ahead — was a gas-giant planet. From the rear of the ship was something that looked to Jobs like a small sun. It glowed with a brilliance that would have blinded and burned them all if not for the goo suits.

But it wasn't a sun at all. The intense color and power and heat were all the result of the ship's engines firing with an outrageous energy.

Jobs looked ahead again. Now, in the gas-giant planet, there appeared a hole, a portal, a gateway, like someone or something had bored through the gigantic mass. The planet was like an apple with its core neatly removed.

And at that moment Jobs realized they were too late to deliver Amelia's message.

"I think Billy is changing course!" Jobs shouted, though he knew nobody could hear him.

He could see Kubrick mouthing some words at him. Mo'Steel, too. Tamara's eyes seemed to be fixed on the tunnel ahead.

And then — in half a second, in a fraction of a heartbeat, in no time at all, as though Mother were no larger or heavier than a dart being thrown at a corkboard, the ship shot ahead toward the planet and into the hole, dragging Jobs, Mo'Steel, Kubrick, and Tamara with it.

Violet drew her sweater closer around her. Burroway had asked for a chilly, overcast afternoon. Weather appropriate for a funeral. It was the first official burial service the Remnants had held since waking up on board the ship. T.R. was the first of their dead to be so honored.

They stood around the Victorian-style mausoleum Billy had provided at Olga's suggestion. She had said a few remembered words.

Violet glanced at 2Face, standing a few feet away, eyes on the ground. Oddly, 2Face had been silent during the brief service. Since she'd come back from seeing Billy, she'd been sort of quiet overall.

But Violet didn't have time to think about what might be going on with 2Face. Because a deep shudder under her feet made her stumble. Dr. Cohen reached out and steadied herself against the wall of the mausoleum. D-Caf grasped Roger Dodger. Olga and Noyze crouched down on the damp grass. 2Face reached for Edward, her eyes suddenly bright.

It's happening, Violet thought, momentarily stunned, disbelieving. *It's actually happening. We're going home.*

K.A. APPLEGATE

REMNANTS™

⑨

No Place Like Home

"HALF HUMAN. HALF SOMETHING ELSE."

"I need butter," Edward said.

"What's the magic word?" Olga asked.

"Please," Edward said automatically.

Jobs shook his head and smiled as he passed the butter to his brother. The scene was weird. Weird on many levels. Weird that Olga was teaching table manners to a kid who had taken on the coloration of his chair until he was almost invisible. Weird that they were eating "steak" and "spinach soufflé" off fine china when they knew the Meanies could attack any second. Weird that a strangely two-dimensional maid was busy refilling their water glasses.

Violet had organized this dinner to cheer everyone up, but so far it was a gloomy affair.

Mo'Steel was out of sorts because Noyze and Dr. Cohen were AWOL. He'd been the first to notice they were nowhere in The Zone. Everyone knew they must have gone off to talk to the Meanies about peace. Mo'Steel wasn't the type to worry, but Jobs had a feeling Mo'Steel was mad Noyze hadn't told him where she was going.

But they weren't talking about that.

"Your centerpiece is beautiful," Olga told Violet.

"Thank you," Violet said. "The shuttle's computer contains an unabridged botanical encyclopedia. I had some fun mixing summer and winter blossoms. An arrangement like this could never exist on Earth. What do you think, Jobs?"

"I was thinking about the Meanies," Jobs said. "Why do you think they're so opposed to heading toward Earth? Where do you want to go?"

Violet sighed. "I said what do you *think* not what are you *thinking*."

"Sorry," Jobs mumbled.

"No shop talk," Violet said. "You promised."

Jobs looked down at his plate. Trying to relax now was like trying to relax on a plummeting airplane. His mind couldn't let go of the fact he was facing death. Worries about the Meanies, Honey

Roach, Noyze, Dr. Cohen, and this Charlie guy kept popping up and demanding attention.

The silence stretched out until Jobs shifted nervously in his chair. He fished for some piece of inoffensive small talk. Came up empty.

"It's Amelia I don't understand," Olga finally said. "Sorry, Violet. But I just keep thinking she'd welcome a chance to check out Earth. Same as us. She's human, same as us."

"Well, not exactly," Mo'Steel said. "Not anymore. Amelia is more like the X-Men. Half human. Half something else. A mutant."

Olga smiled "And I thought all that time you spent reading p-comics was a waste."

Violet sighed again and motioned for the maid to remove their plates. They were half full. The food Billy/Mother created was always slightly off. Strangely metallic tasting. Jobs didn't have much of an appetite anyway. He was too keyed up.

"Do you think Mother created Amelia?" Mo'Steel asked. "You know, the way she created Kubrick?"

"I don't think so, no," Jobs said. "Billy couldn't find a file on her. Also, remember when we saw her in the basement? She said she was *evolving*."

"One person doesn't evolve," Olga said. "A species evolves."

"Jobs told her that," Mo'Steel said. "It was like a tractor-pull for science geeks. Lots of heavy wrestling over terms."

"One person couldn't evolve on Earth," Violet said. She shot Jobs an unhappy look, acknowledging the fact they were now talking shop. "But the same rules don't apply here. I'm not sure any rules apply."

"Don't forget Amelia said she had help from the greatest force in the universe," Jobs said. "Whatever that's supposed to mean."

"Maybe . . . the Shipwrights?" Olga suggested.

"You think the Shipwrights are the greatest force in the universe?" Jobs asked doubtfully.

"Stronger than the Riders or the Meanies," Olga said. "Who else is around?"

She said it dismissively and everyone looked surprised when Jobs said, "Two possibilities. Either there's simply some condition aboard this vessel that causes mutations to occur — something that acts a little like radiation, for example, or . . ."

"Or what?" Mo'Steel demanded.

Jobs glanced at Edward, but he seemed focused on the slices of blueberry cheesecake the maid was serving. "Or — there's someone else on board

Mother. Someone other than the Meanies and Riders and Shipwrights. Some other species or force."

"What do you mean, force?" Edward asked. So he was listening. Great.

Jobs considered dropping it. Edward didn't need to hear this. And Violet had made him promise to forget, or ignore, their worries for one evening.

But he couldn't seem to shut up. This was important. And he couldn't miss the opportunity to talk things over with the only people he still trusted. Besides, now they were all staring at him. Waiting to hear what he had to say. Even Violet.

"I mean, a force. Someone or some*thing* that lacks the power to act directly but has the power to manipulate others," Jobs said. "The power to change others, mutate them."

"Why?" Mo'Steel asked.

"Yeah," Violet said impatiently. "Why would anyone want to cause mutations?"

Jobs licked his lips. This was the kind of problem he liked best. The simple act of thinking about it soothed him. "Look at the mutations," he said. "What do we know?"

Edward was listening intently now, cheesecake forgotten. "We know I turned into a chameleon."

"Right," Jobs said. Of course Edward was interested. They were talking about him. "We also know Yago has somehow developed — talents that make the Meanies think he's a god. And Billy has a whole bunch of strange powers —"

"There's also the Baby and Tamara," Olga put in.

"And Amelia," Mo'Steel said. "And Kubrick."

"But it's obvious not all of these changes happened in the same way," Olga said. "Edward has changed gradually, seemingly spontaneously. Painlessly. That supports your environmental hypothesis. But Kubrick was altered by Mother physically. Totally different story."

"True," Jobs said. "Just thinking out loud."

"And didn't you tell me Billy had psychic dreams back on Earth?" Violet asked, her irritation clear in her voice. Jobs could tell she didn't want to be having this conversation. "You said he saw the blimps and Rider Ocean before we ever even got on the shuttle."

"True," Jobs said. "It doesn't add up to a neat sequence of causation."

Mo'Steel raised an eyebrow. "Translation."

"I'm puzzled," Jobs said with a shrug. "It's a mystery."

"The Baby and Tamara don't fit into any pattern, either," Olga said. "The Baby was born sometime during our journey. Presumably he was already partly a Shipwright before the shuttle encountered Mother. Another mutant."

"Maybe there is no connection," Jobs said. "It's just — only a handful of people exists here and a good proportion of them have altered or have *been* altered. That may be totally random or it may not. I just think it's worth looking for connections."

"Yago changed the same way I did," Edward said. "I mean, nobody noticed."

A connection clicked inside Jobs' mind and he smiled. "Here's an interesting observation. Yago's and Edward's mutations are similar in another way. They mirror their personalities. Edward is a quiet kid" — Edward was more than quiet; he was practically invisible. Even back on Earth he had made few demands and gotten little attention — "and his mutation heightens that personality trait. Same with Yago."

"He was always the center of the universe in his own mind," Violet said with a strange smile. "And now he's like a pop star walking through a junior high cafeteria. Only instead of being surrounded by twelve-year-old girls, his fans are aliens."

Jobs nodded. "Amelia might be the same way. We don't know anything about her. It's possible she was — *diseased*, back on Earth."

"I still wouldn't call it a mutation," Olga said. "What Amelia can do — turning the bacteria and fungi in her body into a weapon — that's just too far out. Human DNA can only be twisted so far."

Jobs nodded thoughtfully. "Olga's right. DNA is analog. You can twist it only so many ways. Some person or some force is treating human beings as if they were digital — just so many databits to be added or subtracted or recombined."

"That's not evolution," Olga said.

"So forget the word *evolution*," Jobs said easily. "Forget the word *mutation*. Call it a redesign or a re-imagining. The important thing is to understand what's happening. Someone or something is manipulating at least some of our bodies. And maybe all of them."

"And you're saying these . . . these rewrites, these fundamental changes — may reflect some preexisting character trait?" Violet said.

Jobs shrugged. "Sure, maybe, I don't know."

"You're speculating?" Violet demanded.

"Absolutely," Jobs said.

"Well, I don't know about the rest of you, but I've had enough speculation for one evening," Violet said, her tone icy.

"Violet —" Job started. He was beginning to regret breaking his promise to her. They were all tired and worried. Maybe Violet needed a break more than he realized.

Violet waved him off. "You relax by examining things, trying to explain them. Not everyone is the same way."

"I know," Jobs said miserably.

"Well." Olga stood up and smiled bravely. "Thanks for a lovely evening, Violet. And thank you, Jobs, for a provocative conversation. I'd better be going now."

Violet got up, too. "I think I'll come with you," she said.

Jobs tried to catch Violet's eye, to send her a look that said he was sorry. But Violet was careful not to look in his direction.